Deep Diving

Cate Ellink

EasyRead Large

Copyright Page from the Original Book

ISBN: 9780857991829

Title: Deep Diving

www.escapepublishing.com.au

TABLE OF CONTENTS

Deep Diving
Cate Ellink

From Cate Ellink comes a sun-soaked, sandy, seaside erotic novel about a tropical paradise, two athletes used to getting physical, and a sex-filled, no-strings holiday fling.

Samantha is celebrating her newly retired status from competitive triathlons with a diving holiday in her favourite place in the world: Australia's Lord Howe Island. But all divers need a buddy, and Sam can't dive solo. A chance meeting with rugby league superstar Cooper Sterling in the dive shop seems serendipitous. Sam can't wait to have a partner who might be able to keep up with her.

It soon becomes evident that Cooper and Sam are compatible both in and out of the water, and things gets seriously sexy. But Sam is disinclined to be another football groupie, and Cooper has been burned before. So the rules are clear: a holiday fling, no strings attached, and they part as friends at the end.

But as the final days of their time together come to a close and a life apart becomes a reality, Sam and Cooper start to question their decision. Is this holiday fling really the finish line or can Sam and Cooper turn their friendly competition into more than sizzling sex?

About the Author

Cate Ellink loves scuba diving, snorkelling, photography, holidays on Lord Howe Island, and rugby league. She's not so fond of running or hiking up hills and knows nothing about fame.

Cate's an Eels fan (but don't hold that against her) who spent the 1980s collecting autographs of her favourite players. That's as close as she came to rugby league stars.

Cate lives near the beach in NSW, Australia, with a long-suffering husband. She has one other book with Escape Publishing, *The Virginity Mission,* and has published a few short stories.

You can find out more on her website: www.cateellin k.com

Acknowledgements

I write with a large cast helping me in the background. I can't do without them! Any errors, however, are all my own. Much thanks and appreciation to:

Ainslie Paton, who helped shape this story when I had it mixed up with another at the start, and then when I messed the ending.

Rhyll Biest for giving awesome feedback.

Mel Teshco went chapter by chapter helping me to get my words in order and reducing my repetition.

Stephan Kern encouraged me to write a less timid heroine.

Mervet McClintock has been on my writing journey from the beginning and always offers helpful suggestions.

Many others also support my writing dreams including Sandra Linklater, Judy O'Connor, Anita Joy, Lisa Roderick, Anna Simons, Sheridan Kent, and the other Naughty Ninjas: Lily Malone, Georgina Penney, Andra Ashe, Roz Groves, Sarah Belle and Sandra Antonelli.

I would never be published without the support of the Romance Writers of Australia, and the erotic group of authors.

Escape Publishing and Kate Cuthbert who take a chance on my stories, and Julia Knapman for being a fabulous editor and picking up thousands of repetitions and silly things.

My Dad, Jim. He's a constant support to my writing and my life. He assures me I can't shock him—hope this one doesn't either, Dad!

My sisters, their families, and my friends who have always put up with my craziness.

My Aunty Faye, Uncle Len, my cousin Wendy and her husband Andreas, for an afternoon of chatting about erotic writing without embarrassment.

Rugby League. I've been a fan since I was a kid (go the mighty Eels!). Two number sevens have caught my imagination—one in the 80s and one now. My hero was inspired by these men. I thank them for their contribution to my life, even though I've never met them (and they'd probably find it creepy!).

My husband. He's survived another book, more conversations about sex, hours of football, and competed for my time against my imaginary hero—thank you for being by my side.

My Dad, Jim, who introduced me to Rugby League

Dear Reader,

I love sports. I'm not great at them but I enjoy lots of different kinds. I've been a rugby league fan for a long time and while watching the 2012 grand final, I was captivated by the winning team's halfback. He's a genius, always busy up front or behind the scenes and then has these pinpoint-accurate end of play kicks. I started to wonder, how could you meet someone like him? And could you help falling in love?

I've never met him, and I know next to nothing about him, but over the last year I've invented my version of Cooper, Samantha's hero. Although I've borrowed a body and a job, everything is a figment of my imagination. And the fact that I wrote a lot of this story while watching footy games is just a bonus.

Samantha and I have little in common. She came about because a friend told me I needed to write a 'kickass' heroine and not another girl with doubts. Sam's got a few misgivings because I couldn't get rid of mine completely! But I hope she's worthy of Cooper, and vice versa.

I've enjoyed the trip to Lord Howe Island, one of my favourite places, with Sam and Cooper. I hope you'll enjoy it too.

With my best wishes,
Cate xo

Chapter 1

My wolf-whistle cuts through the morning stillness, loud, shrill and penetrating. The stranger doesn't turn. His stride shortens for one step but that's the only indication he's heard me. A smile sneaks across my mouth, twisting as I try to stop it from blooming into a full laugh. I've got no class.

I'm perving. Hidden behind sunglasses, squinting in the sunshine, I'm availing myself of the unexpected addition to an already stunning view. I usually go for long, lean athletes. This guy is stocky but he's definitely an athlete. Muscles upon muscles, layered and sculpted to perfection. His gait is long and easy. He's about my height but built like a brick outhouse, as my pop would have said. A very attractive one if the rear is anything to go by. He has huge calves, thick flexing thighs, and tight butt cheeks rounding out his shorts decadently. How would my hand go curving around those gluteus maximuses, or is it maximi in pairs? I'd need both hands for sure. They twitch, palms sweating, fingers wriggling, eager to close in on their target.

He's alone and heading towards the dive shack, like me. I hope he's solo. I wouldn't mind him for a dive buddy. I'd have some delicious moments of viewing pleasure.

I follow him into the building where we both check in. After giving my name, Samantha Caine, I turn towards him immediately. 'Hi. I'm Sam. How you doing?' I extend my hand.

He smiles and the air hitches in my throat. Beautiful white teeth, double dimples on the left, single on the right, smile lines fanning from gleaming brown eyes. His head tips marginally to the right. Our handshake lodges the breath firmly in my throat—rough flesh rubs against my palm as thick, strong fingers detain mine.

'I'm doing well, thanks. I'm Cooper Sterling. Nice to meet you, Sam.' His voice makes my bones melt. Thank God for my sunglasses. I'm seriously hiding behind them now.

He gives me back my hand and a gasp spills out in a hurry. 'You too.' We stand in awkward silence for a moment. My wits are scattered and I need time to gather them. I don't fluster like this. I've been around too many attractive men to act like a goofy teenager. A woman's voice from outside the dive shack has me collecting myself quickly. I buddied with her yesterday and I don't want to again. I don't appreciate diving when my buddy, my underwater safety check, leaves me alone in the water.

'Been diving here before, Cooper?'

'No. My first visit to Lord Howe Island. You?'

'I've been a few times.' I laugh softly before admitting, 'More than a few. I don't bother going anywhere else. This place has claimed my soul.'

'It's that good?' He smiles as he questions, with eyebrows lifting. His face is chiselled angles and planes, with fine eyebrows and chocolate eyes. Not classically beautiful but broad, square and attractive.

'I think so. But then I like coloured fish, coral, diving and snorkelling. I also like being able to walk around and feel safe, even at night.'

'You're on your own?' At my nod, he says, 'Me too.'

'Oh.' I hesitate for just a moment, wondering if I should ask, but hell, life's there for the risk-takers, not nancy-girls. 'Are you looking for a buddy?' I pause again, thinking I should add more but unsure of what it should be.

'Yeah, I am, but I'm not a great buddy. I like to take my time, look at the little things.' He has thick brown hair that overhangs his forehead and softens his face. His lips are plump and dusky pink on a mouth that looks like it easily smiles. Curves dip at the edges, not quite dimples at the moment, making him look friendly. If he stays anywhere close, I'll enjoy watching him. He's solid as well as cute.

'Sounds like my kind of diving. I'm not after competition, I'm an explorer.'

He holds out his hand. 'Looking forward to diving with you then, Sam.' When I slip my hand in his, it's dwarfed and a warmth spreads along my arm. For a moment I bask in that wonderful sensation of being surrounded and comforted. And then I squeeze his hand slightly and whip out a charming smile. I keep these smiles especially for men who know they're hot and expect you to fall at their feet. It makes them think you're not immune. His confidence is huge. I need to control my reaction to him, or I'll look like an easy sexual conquest. Before I can say anything, he speaks.

'There's one condition I have for my dive buddy.' He pauses until I look at him. He's staring intently at me, his eyes almost sparkling, making me think he's going to say something sexy and smart. 'No wolf-whistles. It's uncool.'

I burst out laughing. 'Yeah, I can be like that. I'll try not to let the uncoolness out again. Shall we go get our gear?'

For the briefest moment his eyes widen at my blasé attitude. I guess he wanted me to repent or squirm but I don't. I secretly grin. He recovers quickly and follows me towards the side shed where the gear's stored.

My off-hand attitude's got me out of tricky situations. People think I'm not smart, or easily pushed around, and then I hit them with an unsuspecting move—like shrugging off a concern or taking control of a dive partnership. Men like Cooper expect to be in control. They don't realise that I do too.

'I'm from Adelaide. I take it you're from Australia too?' His accent is Australian, so I'm guessing he's from the mainland.

'Melbourne.' Short and sharp.

I'm not going to let it worry me. 'Oh, I grew up there.' He doesn't follow my lead so I don't push the subject. That's fine. I'll stick to diving.

While we're collecting gear, I ask him about the underwater signals he's accustomed to and we run through them. He has no hesitation in chatting about diving.

Armed with our scuba kit, we assemble it and load onto the boat. Once everyone's aboard it's only a short trip to the dive site, Erscotts Hole.

The brief from Brian, the divemaster, is quick but thorough and Cooper nods in the appropriate places. He seems to be serious about his diving, which gives me confidence that he may be an okay buddy. Useful, not just pretty.

When our gear's donned and we've done our buddy checks, we're given the nod that it's our turn to enter the water.

'Good diving, Sammy,' Cooper says as he takes the giant stride entry into the water. I roll my eyes. *Sammy. Excellent.* Calling me that makes me feel 15, not 38. I know I don't act my age and I don't look it, but ... *Sammy?* I shake my head. My taking the lead is not going to be easy, but I love a challenge.

Holding the regulator in my mouth with the heel of my hand, and my mask tight to my face with spread fingers, I take the giant stride entry too. The cool water finds every way to enter the wetsuit and chill me. I surface, shivering. I give the okay signal to the boat.

Cooper has his regulator out of his mouth and speaks as soon as I turn to him. 'All okay?' After I nod, he frowns. His eyes squint and his nose crinkles behind the mask. 'Are you cold?'

That he notices surprises me. That he asks, more so. 'I'm fine. Just water seeping in.'

He chuckles a rich, delicious sound that makes me shiver for all the wrong reasons. 'You should warm up soon, but let me know if you don't and we'll go back early.'

I nod, incapable of speech. He'd cut the dive short if I was cold? If that's true, he's going to be some buddy.

I signal that I'm ready to descend and he nods. My regulator is popped in my mouth and I give it a pulse of air. All working right. Then I expel air from my buoyancy control device. Fins pointing downward, we begin the slow drop into the mystical underwater world. The water is crisp and visibility clear. We watch each other as we make our descent. He smiles as I equalise multiple times, making sure my ears don't hurt as the water pressure increases. The water changes to a bright aqua and then a deeper blue. It's beautiful. The descent is easy and Cooper stays within my vision.

Eight metres later we reach the sandy bottom. In the time it takes for me to snort again to unblock my ears, lots of fish come out for the greeting, colourful wrasse darting around me, zooming towards my mask. I look over at Cooper, half expecting him to be gone but he's there, his eyes dancing behind his mask as he plays with the fish.

We give each other an okay signal concurrently. He reaches out and taps against the wetsuit covering my forearm. I look at him, wondering what he wants. He crosses his arms and rubs his hands up and down his upper arms. *He's cold?* Then he points at me, and turns his hand over asking the question. Smiling so hard my reg nearly pops out of my mouth, I shake my head and give an okay. I'm all warm now, even more so after he's remembered to ask.

He indicates the rock shelf and when I give an affirmative, he swims off. His legs make slow kicks that propel him forward easily. Suspended in the deep blue, expelling few bubbles, he seems at home. I wonder how long he's been diving. He looks comfortable. He turns his head and his body flips half over. Hand open again, he questions me—aren't I coming? I kick off and swim beside him, almost tempted to lay my hand on his outstretched palm. I have a buddy who gives a hoot. An unexpected change.

When I reach the rock ledge, a loud exclamation spills from me. Nudibranchs, my favourite marine creature. They're the most gorgeous slug-like creatures made beautiful by brightly coloured frills and squat spikes that flutter in the current. Even though they're tiny, they catch my attention. I spend too long ogling them. Feeling guilty, I look around for Cooper and he's there, about two metres away, examining nudibranchs and soft corals on the rocks. Fish dart around him as his fingers stir up sediment from the rocks. Like me, he doesn't wear gloves and touches everything.

Beyond the large rock Cooper's touching, a moray eel weaves its way from a rock cave. From where Cooper is, I don't think he'll be aware of the eel and I don't want it biting him by mistake. I touch his arm and make an upwards weaving motion with my hand and point. He frowns, looks to where I pointed, then his eyes widen and he grins. He gives me an okay. He moves over the hole and then backs away. The moray edges upwards and peers around. We wait, watching the eel tentatively weave from its cave.

'Beautiful.' You shouldn't be able to hear underwater but some people are clear, like Cooper. I distinctly hear him even through bubbles and water.

'I know.' I nod. Before we move away, I check my air gauge and show it to Cooper. He mirrors my action. We have about the same amount of air left, three quarters of a tank, so we should both be ready to finish the dive around the same time. It's annoying to have a buddy who chews through their air and your dive is much shorter than expected because you have to return to the surface.

We keep exploring the rock ledge. No other divers are in view, it's like we have the world to ourselves. It's been a long time since I've been relaxed and comfortable enough with a buddy to spend time exploring the little things. Further along, Cooper stops and holds up his hand. I come up beside him. Suspended in the water I wait to see what has caught his attention. His arm moves slowly, his hand held into a decisive point as he directs my gaze to the left. I follow the line from his long, thick fingers but can't see anything out of the ordinary. I know it's nothing scary because Cooper is relaxed. But a part of me thinks he'd be relaxed even if it were a huge shark. He has a confidence about him. A competency and calmness that exudes, along with his warmth, beyond his wetsuit.

He turns to me and I frown, shrugging and holding my hands open in question. He smiles, eyes dancing again, and holds one hand flat in front of his chest, then draws the other hand in an arc over his hand. *A turtle?*

I look again at where he pointed. Jagged rocks, waving corals. My eyes drift across and back, scanning to see it. I drop my gaze to the bottom of the ledge and there, tucked beneath a waving frond is a rounded rock, but not a rock. Too smooth to be a rock. I drift to the bottom and lie on the sand. The rounded rock pokes its head around and a dark eye stares at me, blinks once, and turns towards Cooper. Another blink. Lying on the bottom with our small drift of air bubbles racing to the surface, we pose no threat to it. With an ungainly flick of large flippers, it lifts from the bottom and drifts out before swimming across in front of us. It must be half a metre long.

'Oh God.' My voice holds such awe I wonder if Cooper can hear me.

As the turtle glides past, I caress the edge of its shell, shivering with excitement. Cooper's large fingers brush against the shell alongside mine. I turn towards him, grabbing onto his arm, and I wonder if my eyes are as wide as his. I take my reg out and mouth a 'wow' before popping it back in to breathe. Cooper nods. 'Amazing.' Again, his voice is clear. This is the magical underwater world at its greatest. We watch the turtle swim away until we can no longer see it.

When the turtle's gone, the rock wall, fish, corals, even the nudibranchs are almost dull. I check my air and it's time to head back. I tap Cooper's hand and show him my gauge. He nods; he has the same amount of air and it's time to go.

We head back to the boat. At the chain for the buoy, Cooper and I ascend together. I can't believe what an incredible dive it's been. Even without the turtle I would have been impressed. It's not often I score a buddy who's perfect.

We break the surface with the same reaction, regulators spit from our mouths in the rush to speak.

'Oh God, that was freaking unbelievable.' At the same time Cooper says, 'That was the best dive ever.' We laugh. I'm bobbing on the surface in a bubble of magical happiness. I lie back. The clear blue sky is smattered with cotton balls of white fluff. It is a perfect day, a perfect dive, a perfect buddy.

Cooper has his fins off and tucked under his arm when he taps my forearm. I push my mask back and wipe my eyes.

'You staying here all day?' He nods to the boat. 'They're ready for us.'

'Oh, sorry. You go up first.' I lean down to slide my fins off while I watch him. He explodes from the water like a great dripping black god. I'm mesmerised. The way he effortlessly climbs the ladder and shucks his gear has me gasping for breath.

He vanishes from sight. Luckily, because I doubt I can climb the ladder with his body arresting my attention. Hell. He was hot before, but now he's hot and a great buddy, which means so much more.

I drag myself up the ladder, feeling as if the wetsuit and tank have added 20 kilograms to my usual light frame. In the water, moving is effortless; on land I'm cumbersome with all the gear. I always think of penguins when I'm waddling out of a dive. They glide so effortlessly through the water but look ridiculous on land.

'Here, pass me your fins.' Cooper's voice and his strong hands draw my mind away from penguins. Without looking up, I hand him my fins with my mask and snorkel shoved inside. I waddle onto the boat.

'Thanks.'

I wade over to the air cylinder bench and plonk myself down. And here he is again, best buddy in the world, helping to remove my vest and air cylinder. We take our gear apart, and after I've blown air onto the plastic stopper and finished with the air cylinder, Cooper grabs it and secures it to the boat.

'Thanks, Cooper.' He gives me a wickedly sexy grin and I have to close my eyes and take a few deep slow breaths before I can look at him again. What was in that air? I went from perving to wanting to desperately needing within the space of a dive.

I head to the side of the boat where I stowed my gear, hoping it will give me some Cooper-free sanity. After a dive my mouth is like the bottom of a bird cage. The dry air saps all the moisture, so I always carry a couple of water bottles. I grab one and drink half of it in one go. As I pull it from my mouth a pang of guilt hits me. I had the perfect dive buddy, I should offer him a drink. I lean down to grab the other bottle when I feel the air beside me heat.

The heat could only belong to him. 'Would you like a drink, Cooper?' I ask as I close my hand on the second drink bottle and stand.

He licks his lips and I try not to follow the flick of his tongue, or drool over the shining gleam on his lips. 'No, I'll be right.' I'm sure he's only being polite.

I hand him my second, unopened bottle. 'I always bring a couple. I hate the dry air feeling.' He grabs it with a smile and a nod.

We lean against the side of the boat while we drink. I deliberately don't look at him. I don't want to see him swallowing. I don't want to see moisture on his mouth. I don't want to see his lips close around the top of the drink bottle. My imagination is doing a great job without needing the visual.

Truthfully, I want all those things. I want him. But I know a hundred Coopers. Men with muscles and looks can write their own tickets for women. Women fall over themselves to bed them, partner them, be seen with them. I won't. Not any more. Cooper may not have the long, lean muscles I'm familiar with, but he's the exact same breed and I need to stay clear.

I gulp the rest of my water, hoping it will stop me thinking of his mouth. 'Thanks. I thoroughly enjoyed that dive.'

'The moray was amazing.'

'And the turtle. How did you spot him? He was incredible. I can't believe we touched him.'

'And you don't wear gloves. You touch things?'

I have a strange feeling he means, girls aren't meant to want to touch animals, although maybe that's my issue being projected to his words. 'I like to know what they feel like. I mean, I know how turtles feel at the aquarium but I want to know how they feel really, underwater. Is that crazy?'

'Not to me. That's what I want to know too.' Mutual understanding. Amazing. I push my hair back from my face, running my fingers through the tangled curls, before twisting it into a loose knot to keep it out of the way. I keep it mid-shoulder length so it's easy to tie up and away.

'It's hot and these guys will be a while.' Cooper waves to the couple we're waiting on who surfaced a fair way from the boat and are swimming back, taking their sweet time. He unzips his wetsuit and peels it from his shoulders down his arms. Five-millimetre thick neoprene does not mould and bend easily. It sticks to your flesh and grabs hold, needing an effort to peel it off, and he's tugging hard to remove it. *Holy freaking hell.* His size is not bulk or flesh, but muscle, honed exquisite muscle. Everywhere. Tightly flexed with defined edges begging for my tongue to trace. Solid planes calling for me to lick across their surface. *Mercy.*

I was perving before the dive but I didn't watch him gear up. Thank heavens! I wouldn't have been able to concentrate knowing this was beneath the wetsuit. I hate to think what my expression is, so I scurry behind him on the pretence of helping him peel the wetsuit from his arms and back. But that's a bad move, crazy bad move. My mouth, only just re-moistened, becomes drier than when I was sucking air during the dive. It's difficult to breathe, almost as if each breath is snagged on the ripples of his back. I hold his wetsuit collar, trying not to touch his skin, as he struggles from the sleeves. My hands move down the wetsuit, helping him peel it off, following the body heat which radiates from the wetsuit and pours from his body. I react by flushing. My face is no doubt flaming crimson. Between my breasts, sweat pools.

His bulk shouldn't have me melting. But he's Wolverine solid.

And he'll still have women falling all over him, Sam. The bulk makes no scrap of difference.

'Thanks, Sammy.' His voice drags me from my lust-filled haze. His struggle ends and I drop his sleeves and step beside him. The top of the wetsuit hangs, clinging from his waist. If I keep to his side, surely the muscles won't dance before my eyes, silently calling for my touch. *Sweet hell.*

I grab at my wetsuit zip and tear it down, before struggling to peel the wretched thing down my arms. As I'm wrenching the material down my left arm, Cooper grabs hold and peels it effortlessly from me.

My brain's screaming 'danger' but I'm not listening. I'm reacting. Against my better judgement, I lean into his body while his heat surrounds me. I hold onto his waist as he struggles to pull the right sleeve off. My fingers tingle against the thick muscle that flexes and fills beneath my fingertips. I have seconds bathed in heat before I mentally restrain myself and drag my body away.

Holy freaking hell. The heat from his hands, the expert way he moves me and the wetsuit in opposite directions until I'm divested of everything but my swimming costume, tells me he's well used to undressing women. I'm not surprised.

'Thanks. I never get good buddies like you. Someone taught you exceptionally well.' I chuckle, knowing that I'm flirting but telling myself I can handle it.

He grins that sexy smile he's given me before, where one side of his mouth lifts and his cheek plumps and creases. His eyes get a half-closed look, which reminds me of a post-coital satiated gaze and my stomach takes a rollercoaster ride.

I suck in two breaths of salty air before I turn in his direction. He's peeling his wetsuit down his legs. Thighs better than I remembered emerge. Well-defined, deliciously huge thighs streaked with sinew. His knees are overshadowed by quads swelling with tight ripples. He turns his back as he peels the wetsuit lower. His back flexes as he tries to pull the wetsuit from his ankles. But it's the rounded globes of his butt that hold my gaze. *Oh, dear heaven. What a butt.*

He needs help. Reluctantly I move in front of him, grab the wetsuit and help to pull it over his feet. Wide feet, with broad toes. Feet I'd like to...

Whoa!

This public dive boat is no place for these thoughts to be taken further.

Swathed in a towel, I have my defences up before he returns from taking both wetsuits to the bucket on board. He pulls on shorts and a T-shirt before leaning against the boat rail beside me. I can't decide if I'm glad he's covered up or not. Everyone's on board now, so we head back in.

Continuing flirting would be fun but instead I speak about the dive. 'There were so many fish down there.'

'And so friendly. I don't think I've had fish come up to my face like that.'

'I've been to lots of dive spots but they're much friendlier here. That's why I keep coming back.'

'Do you come here often?' he asks.

'Every year for the past six or so years. I can't stop coming.'

'Why? There are lots of diving holidays.'

I look from the lagoon to the island, the twin peaks to the east, the scooping dip of land in the middle of the island, and to the western hills. My lips twist as I list the reasons. 'The diving here is as good as anywhere else, and the snorkelling is as good as the diving. There are walks if you feel like climbing a hill. And it's safe. I can roam around after dinner and never worry about my safety.' I pause and tip my head to the side. 'And the food's great.'

'Do you always travel alone?'

'I prefer to. I've travelled with friends but it usually ruins the friendship. I've travelled a lot for work, in groups, so holidays alone are important for my sanity.'

He nods in a way that makes me think he understands. 'How long are you here for?'

'Ten more days. You?'

'Two weeks. Each year I do a dive holiday somewhere and I've not been here before. I usually go overseas.'

'Why overseas when there are so many great sites in Australia?'

He shifts as if uncomfortable before shrugging and avoiding my question. 'Would you mind...' He pauses before beginning again. 'Are you doing more dives?'

'Yes, every day, at least one. A night dive tomorrow if they have enough people. You?'

'I haven't booked ahead. I wasn't sure what it'd be like.'

As the boat pulls into the shore, the gangway lowers, and Cooper leans close. His breath drifts over the edge of my ear, down my neck, and skims across my collarbone. Goosebumps cover me. It's delicious.

'Would you mind if I buddied with you for your dives? Or is that too pushy?' He leans back and a cross between a smirk and a smile flits across his face.

A thousand thoughts scramble through my head. I'd like to be cool and say no, but it's game playing and I'm no longer playing those games. He's a great buddy, I can't deny I enjoy his company. My hesitation stems from my attraction. Can I handle myself without falling over him? I pause, running the tip of my tongue along the seam of my lips. Surely I can control myself. 'I'd like that.'

Together we unload and rinse our gear. We work together and chat about the dive while my mind muses. His muscles are huge, he must play footy. He's from Melbourne so it must be AFL, since Victoria is virtually governed by Aussie Rules. But he's kind of short, although what else would he play in

Melbourne? We head to the office to book the rest of the dives.

'Do you play AFL?' I ask Cooper the question as we walk out of the dive shack. It's probably a little impertinent or maybe I should have led into it so it isn't so abrupt but he just chuckles when I ask, as if he expects my directness.

'Not that brand, but football, yes.'

'Hence the muscles.' *Another brand of football, in Melbourne, who would have guessed?*

He laughs. 'Yeah, they're a bit hard to miss, aren't they?' His self-deprecating response makes me smile.

'They kind of hide under a wetsuit.'

He grins and a knowing look appears in his eyes. 'I did notice the effect of removing it.' He lifts his eyebrows quickly and I can only laugh.

I mock-punch his shoulder and immediately regret my action. It's like punching a cement wall. I pull away and rub my knuckles.

'Big mistake, Sammy.' He slides his hand over mine, his fingertips brushing across my knuckles. My gaze locks on the contrast between my small hand and his huge paw. A sensation of warmth floods me again and that's before he leans over and presses his lips to my knuckles. 'That should make it all better.'

Lust tears right through me. My knuckles tingle but my body buzzes. I meet his gaze and the air between us grows hotter. I can hardly draw a breath. In a split second I know I can walk towards him and be lost in him, or I can step back and cool things down.

He's a footballer. Women fall over him all the time.

I step back, dragging my hand away from his grasp. 'Thanks for the dive. I might get going and get some snorkelling in.'

'Where's the best spot to snorkel?'

So much for cooling things down. It doesn't look like I'm going to lose him. We head to town, his steps matching mine. It's a comfortable togetherness even after the heat.

'If you want big fish, Neds Beach is my favourite spot. One of the locals feeds the fish in the afternoon and it's brilliant to snorkel as the fish mill around waiting for him. Big kingfish, tailor, mullet, wrasse, garfish, silver drummer, and spangled emperors are all there. Reef sharks come in too. It's awesome. But hang out the back, you don't want to get into the feeding frenzy because there are people everywhere and it's crazy.'

He's grinning as if it's Christmas and I can't help but offer an invitation. I can imagine his face when he sees it and I want to be there, with him. 'Do you want to grab something to eat and come with me?'

His gaze locks with mine and the heat of a few moments ago returns, making me almost regret my invitation. 'I'd like that. Thanks.' But he doesn't step any closer, he doesn't touch me and we keep to our companionable walk.

I should be pleased but damn it, I want lust swamping me again. It's been a long time since I've felt like that. Cursing myself silently, we make our way to the town centre and food. I hope I don't end up eating him ... well, not today anyway.

Chapter 2

After grabbing sandwiches and drinks, we walk across the island to Neds Beach, munching along the way. There's not a lot of chatter as we fill up but I learn he plays rugby league in Melbourne and travels a lot. When we arrive at Neds, I point to the area in front of the shed. 'That's where the fish feeding happens.' I lead him further up the beach. 'I usually snorkel from here, away from the feeding. It's easy to swim into the back of the channel and get amongst the big fish without the hassle of the crowd.'

'How would you know about the fish feeding ... if you don't pick up a ready-made tour guide?' He gives me a quarter-wattage of that knee-wobbling sexy grin and my legs are only a little jelly-like.

'See the yellow sign in front of the shed? It tells you what time's feeding and warns about the fish eating you.'

'What?'

'People get shocked if fish nibble them, even if they do stand in the water while the fish are being fed. You know, people need warning signs.'

He chuckles, hopefully agreeing with me and not thinking I'm a cynical bitch. We shed our outer clothes, grab snorkels and masks and head for the sea. I try to keep my eyes on the water, the beach, anywhere but his body, in Speedos, beside me. As he walks, muscles ripple across his stomach, shoulders, thighs, calves. Not that they capture my attention in any way. I've seen them before, now I'm immune.

I wish!

'No fins?' He asks as we wade in.

'I don't need them snorkelling. You?'

'Same. But I don't have little feet.'

'My feet aren't little.' I look down and then across at his. Mine are tiny. I've never considered myself small, but standing near him I have to concede to his point. 'My feet don't kick, my legs do.' And since I run, they are fairly powerful. Although, next to his, they could be considered toothpicks.

His gaze lands on the tips of my unpainted toenails, slides slowly along my legs and pauses for too long at the juncture of my thighs, before slipping up over my breasts. His stare could be lasers, it burns. Every thought in my brain is fried, except there's a surge of pride. My legs, delineated by long muscles, have been deliberately accentuated by high cut swimmers. I have a waist that pulls in snug beneath my ribs. My breasts, not large, are enhanced by a brightly-coloured bikini top. There's a part of me that preens beneath his gaze, knowing I've worked hard to achieve a body that still looks good in a bikini.

'Do they have a nude beach here?'

His question throws me. 'Ah ... no ... I don't think so. Why?'

'Just thought you'd look better without the bikini.'

Laughing, I wade out quickly until I can dive into the water, hoping it'll cool me down. The mask and snorkel are in my hand, not on my face, but I don't care. I swim until it's deep and then I deal with the gear.

He's definitely trouble. Athletic, cute, flirtatious and funny.

Cooper comes up beside me, his warmth moving along me like a caress. Splashes break the surface as kingfish, some a metre or more in length, circle us. It doesn't take long for Cooper to be attracted to the fish.

A nude beach. That would be great for my 'keeping distance' plan. It's worse knowing the physical attraction is mutual.

The snorkelling is as incredible as I promised. Cooper is like a child ogling presents; eyes round, grin so wide his snorkel can only be held in by his teeth. I never get tired of snorkelling here. After we've snorkelled for ages and swum around the milling fish waiting for their feed, we wade out.

It's his stretch that does my mind in. He drops his snorkelling gear and, before grabbing a towel, stretches his arms up and then folds his hands behind his head. My tongue glues itself to the roof of my mouth. My gaze is gummed to his huge expanse of chest and upper arms. *Frigging hell. He looked big before but now he's freaking humungous.* Tiny tight dark nipples punctuate the wide sweeping pectorals. Knots formed by the thickest rope bulge from his arms. A dark smudge inhabits each armpit, which only enhances the paler surrounding muscles and makes my mouth water. A few stray hairs nestle into the cleft of his chest between pecs. *Oh, to lie against that. To run my tongue across...*

His stomach flexes as he arches backwards. Muscles bulge and press through taut flesh like cobblestones. The tiniest hint of dark hair lies on the navel to cock trail. I refuse to allow my gaze to follow the line. Water droplets sparkle on him.

'Sammy, that was incredible. I don't think I'd have come here without you. Thanks.' His voice is a slightly higher pitch than his usual deep tone, and a little thready as if he's out of breath, but it's more likely a result of the excitement or the stretch. He's so fit I can't ever imagine him panting.

'It's incredible, isn't it? It's my favourite snorkelling spot in the world.' I'm proud that I sound normal.

'No wonder. Fish that size make me drool. Imagine eating them. I'm starving.'

'You must be permanently starving to feed those muscles.' Laughing, I wave my hand up and down in the air, indicating his physique. My fingers tingle, wishing I could be actually touching, not wittily commenting on it.

'I'm only starving when I'm over-active and not well-fed. And you make me active.'

'But you had lunch.' I go to mock-punch him but pull back before I can hurt my hand again.

'Two sandwiches? Not enough in that for me. I need something like that big kingfish.' He pats his stomach and my mouth dries. 'You don't seem to have any trouble keeping up with me.' His comment drips with suggestion, or maybe it's the way his naked gaze flicks over me and every cell in my body feels it and responds. My lips part, gasping for breath.

'I keep pretty active still. To me retirement didn't mean giving up sport and fitness.'

'You're retired?' His words are said with a mixture of confusion, disbelief and maybe a touch of embarrassment, although I could be misreading him. I don't expect everyone to know who I am but I did think a fellow athlete may have recognised me.

'I'm not in my 60s. I retired from international competition. I still do local comps.'

'International competition? What do you do?' At least he sounds impressed.

I try not to react to his lack of knowledge or recognition but my arms fold across my chest. 'Triathlete.'

'Holy shit. No wonder you can keep up with me. I'm impressed.'

I smile, unable to think of a response, witty or otherwise.

I change the subject. 'So, diving tomorrow?' I rub myself briskly with a towel before dragging on a shield of clothes. I lean forward and gather my hair up, twisting it to tie in a loose bun.

Cooper's voice is low as he says my name, before his finger brushes against my nape. The hair along my neck and spine stands on end. My body's caught in suspended time. 'You're sunburned.' His hand curls below my hair. The heel beneath one ear, fingertips under the other. 'And blushing.'

With my lips twisting into a grin, I manage to say, 'You're flirting.' I straighten and look right at him.

'Why wouldn't I? You're reacting.'

'So if I stop reacting, you'll stop flirting?' A lazy grin punctuates my question.

He chuckles. 'Not likely.' He grins and nudges me with his elbow. 'How about dinner?' When I hesitate, he clarifies the invitation. 'I'm starving. It's a no-strings-attached meal. I want to hear about triathlons.'

'Sure. When?' I can talk about competing until the sun comes up and with a fellow athlete, it'll be interesting to compare notes.

'On our way home, unless you have plans.'

'I don't have plans. All I plan are my dives, the rest of the holiday is how it comes.' I get to my feet and grab my gear.

'So, where's the best place to eat?' We walk across the sand, heading for the road.

'Aunty Sue's.' It's an easy answer, my favourite place to eat, with fresh, fabulous food. 'I'm covered in salt, I'd like a shower first.'

Cooper grins. 'You have to be quick. I'm not waiting hours for my food.'

'I won't keep you from your food. Promise.' My fingers brush against his forearm as it swings with his stride. My fingertips are scorched, my palm tingles, and cells dance. Heat suffuses. I need to keep away from his body.

'So where's the restaurant? The other side of the island?' Cooper's question makes me grin. More concerned with food than flirting, that makes a change.

'No, it's at the top of the hill. Along Anderson's Road, almost opposite the Broken Banyan apartments. Do you know where I mean?'

'No. I'm on the other side.'

While we walk my mind's going a hundred miles an hour. I'm at those apartments and I could offer him the use of my shower but he has no clothes to change into. Surely he'll be keen to rinse the salt away? And at this moment, he's more interested in food than sex so he won't misconstrue my invitation. Will he? I doubt it. Besides, I've handled much pushier men than him. 'I'm at the Broken Banyan apartments. If you don't want to walk down and back up, you can use my shower.'

It takes a few seconds for him to examine my invitation. 'Are my shorts and T-shirt okay for the restaurant?' No sexual overtones.

'Sure. It's relaxed, casual. You'll be fine.'

His thanks is delivered with a low-wattage smile.

We turn into the apartment complex and make our way to mine. It's small and isolated, which is why I stay here, but with Cooper beside me it goes from small to tiny.

The key slips into the lock and turns with a growl. It hadn't growled this morning.

Cooper chuckles behind me. 'Sorry. I told you I was starving.'

'That's your stomach, not my door? Phew.' I open the door and invite him in. The apartment has a kitchen-lounge room taking up the majority of the area, and a large bedroom and bathroom to the side.

'We'd better make the showers quick, I don't want you feeding on me for dinner.' I grin what I hope is saucy, cheeky and fun. Before he can answer, I toss my snorkelling gear into the kitchen sink. 'Leave your gear here. I'll wash it and bring it down in the morning.'

'You don't have to do that.'

I shrug. 'There's not much point you lugging it to dinner. It won't take long.'

Stepping into the bedroom, I grab the spare towel and toss it to Cooper. 'You go first while I get some clothes out.' I point him towards the ensuite. As I open the wardrobe, my hand falls on a light green sundress that goes well with my tan. Before I can take it off the hanger, the shower's running. Seems hunger is the more important driver.

***

At the restaurant, after being greeted warmly by the waitress, a loaf of bread and a bottle of water are placed on the table as we're seated. The bread is warm and flavoured with herbs. I can't stop myself. I break off a thick chunk before passing the basket to Cooper. He grabs a piece and bites into it. His lips close over the crust and sink down. His eyes close. Crumbs nestle in the corner of his lips. I want to lean over and lick them up but as soon as I think it, his tongue flicks out and captures them. He swallows the bread, his neck bobbing as he does, and then he slides his tongue across his lips to capture other crumbs that cling.

I squirm on my seat. This is going to be a challenging meal. If I manage not to leave behind a puddle or have a heart attack trying to stop an orgasm, I'll be surprised.

'What's wrong with your bread?' Cooper nods to my hand.

I haven't eaten the bread. After hastily tearing off a chunk it's sitting between my fingers halfway to my mouth in suspended animation. I'm not hungry, at least not for food.

I pour water with my free hand and gulp half a glass before I eat my bread. I can do this. I can flirt and lure without fucking him, at least on the first night. He won't expect resistance. I could make this fun, a competition.

The young waitress has eyes for Cooper. She comes to take our order and looks directly at him. 'What can I offer you tonight?' she asks. I almost choke. Cooper deflects by allowing me to order first. I choose the seafood chowder and Cooper orders blue swimmer crabs. If you're on an island, might as well make use of the seafood.

The waitress completely ignores me. I hope she wrote down my order. Cooper is in her sights. 'Oh, you'll love the crabs. They're fresh today and just to die for. I'll make sure you get the best ones.'

Cooper continues eating his bread as if he hasn't heard her. A brisk nod is all the acknowledgment he gives and I think that's only from politeness.

'Could I recommend a wine?' she asks.

After we both decline wine, the waitress fills our water glasses, leaning over far too much to fill Cooper's. He must have an uninterrupted view down her blouse at a no-doubt lacy bra and spilling breasts.

But he remains motionless, his attention still on me, and she leaves. I'd like to preen or whoop but I sit still until Cooper raises his glass. I do the same.

'To a great dive buddy,' he says, as if the interlude with the waitress had not occurred.

'And great diving.' We clink glasses. My gaze catches with his and the world stops for a few seconds. Scents of salt, yeasty bread and Cooper fill me, magnified in the stillness. The earthy scent of the surrounding rainforest drifts in, mingling with the rich smells of cooking. Our locked gazes snap apart and the world resumes.

'You don't drink wine?' Cooper asks.

'After a misspent youth, I avoid alcohol. You?'

He shakes his head. 'The same.' There's a pause before he says, 'How often do you come here?' And I know he means the restaurant.

'Oh, gosh, I hate to think. Maybe every second night or so.'

'Aren't the other places any good?'

'Oh they are. But I keep coming back here. It lures me every night, which is why I stay so close.'

'I can't believe you're such a foodie.'

'Why not?'

My body flutters beneath the look he skims over me. My sundress no longer covers enough flesh. Breasts swell and press out of my bodice. My arms are too bare, the straps too thin. I'm glad we're seated because the dress would surely be too short even though it skims my knees.

'You must work hard.'

I laugh. 'Are you politely implying I eat too much?' I'm not offended, just teasing.

He flushes a delicate shade of pink that shouldn't suit a man but does him. 'Most women I know don't eat much. I like that you do.'

'I work hard and burn up food. I'm lucky that way. Do you have a strict diet?'

'When I'm training I do. Not so much on holidays but I love fresh food so it's pretty easy.' He lifts his eyes as an older waitress lowers a huge bowl before me. 'Wow. That's the chowder?'

I nod, eyes gleaming. I love the chowder.

Cooper's crabs and salad are on a plate the size of a platter. The young waitress brings them over and fusses around placing them before him. She bends extra low, no doubt luring him with another view of her ample cleavage. Not that I'm jealous or anything.

When he again pays her no attention, it's pretty hard not to inwardly gloat.

He whistles softly when we're alone again. 'You aren't wrong about the size of the meals. There has to be three crabs in this pile.'

'Lucky you're hungry.' I grin, thinking that it would need at least three crabs to fill him up. There's so much of him and not much in a crab.

We tuck into our meals and the conversation drops to minimal. A few moans of pleasure escape me as I hoe into the steaming bowl of chowder. Cooper makes a couple of comments about the fresh, salty taste of his meal. There's not a lot of talking when the food's this good.

About halfway through my chowder, I stop to see how his meal is going. He's the picture of enjoyment as he lifts a forkful of crab flesh, rocket, cherry tomato and cucumber to his mouth. His lips open, a stray rocket leaf snags at the corner and his tongue whisks it inside. Low down my stomach clenches and I clamp my legs tight together. He chews. His eyes widen as he sees my glance and his lips lift at the corners. When he finishes his mouthful, he grins. 'Bloody fantastic.'

I laugh and dig into my chowder. I have to eat and not watch.

The next time I look, his hand is curved around a front nipper and he's trying to snap it open, watching the claw as he pushes his hands towards each other and down. He stares with avid concentration. He seems intent on judging the exact pressure needed to snap it. The tip of his tongue presses against the corner of his mouth, bright pink against his darker lips. His attention is solely focussed on his task, making me wonder if he's like that with his sport. With a resounding snap, the shell breaks and he becomes aware of my gaze. He grins triumphantly. 'This is spectacular.' Then he closes his mouth around one half of the crab claw and sucks.

It's a wicked sight.

His lips hold tightly to the red and white claw. His cheeks dip as he sucks the flesh. Eyes downcast, his lashes lie decadently against high cheekbones. His expressions show at least three of the seven deadly sins—gluttony, greed and lust. Heat races through me and moisture pools between my thighs. God, what would those lips feel like sucking my flesh like that?

Turning his attention to the second half, it slips between his lips and he draws the meat out. As his lips tighten around the crab claw, various body parts within me contract as if his lips were sucking on them. My nipples squeeze tight, throbbing, but nowhere near as hard as my clit. My toes curl into the floor. I shift in my seat, searching for my discarded shoes as if wearing them will halt my reactions.

His eyes widen, his gaze lifts, the empty claw is laid on the plate. He chews on the morsel of flesh. He looks at me and in about two seconds has read my mind. 'I should be glad you aren't the one sucking these claws.' He winks and I choke on air. The rest of the crab legs are devoured while my gaze remains on my chowder. *God, how can I resist him?*

He's interested and why shouldn't he be? I'm still a good catch. Tanned, tall, fit, active. So what if I'm a decade or more older? Although, those added years should give me far more sense. I know sports stars have women falling off them. If they aren't hot for their muscles, then they're hot for the fame that comes from being seen with them. It's not only women affected. I had my share of men after me until I realised it wasn't me they were competing for. I was interchangeable with any other successful female athlete.

Dinner finishes and I manage not to orgasm while Cooper sucks every last crab claw and leg. There must have been hundreds of them. I almost scraped through the china of the chowder bowl trying not to watch. I regaled him with every Olympic tale I could think of to keep my mind off jumping him.

After he's licked each finger clean, the young waitress appears, late and flustered, with a finger bowl. No doubt she's been enjoying the show as much as I have. 'Can I offer you dessert?' she asks breathlessly, her gaze only for Cooper. I try not to cough as I breathe in the innuendo-soaked air.

'No thanks. I don't do dessert.' His comment is light and delivered with no care. I choke on a sip of water. My mind is doing the 'crash and burn' scene from *Top Gun.* I'm glad it wasn't me on the receiving end of his coldness.

When she leaves, I can't help but ask. 'You don't do dessert?'

He shakes his head in a 'not now' kind of way, and asks if I'm finished and ready to go. We argue over the bill before I pay half.

On the way back to my apartment, he says, 'Sorry about the dessert thing.'

'Hey, don't worry. I guess that happens to you a lot.'

He flicks his head around to stare at me, a puzzled look on his face. 'Why do you say that?'

Laughing, shaking my head, and trying not to trip over my feet while I stare at him, I realise he's not being funny. 'Cooper, watching you eat is sinful. Every waitress no doubt wishes you'd eat them for dessert.'

He looks genuinely surprised. 'Sinful? Eating?' He shakes his head and walks on a bit before stopping and turning back to me. 'Feel like a walk?'

'Yes. I often do after a big meal.'

'Where do you walk?'

'Anywhere at all. You pick.'

We walk back to Neds Beach in silence. It's not uncomfortable but I wish I hadn't made that crack about him being sinful.

'Why do you think I'm sinful?' He asks the question as if he can read my thoughts.

'I'm sorry. I shouldn't have said that.'

'Because it's not true, or because you don't want to explain yourself?' He smiles to take the edge off his words but I still feel the sting.

'I don't want to explain myself.' To lighten the solemn mood I add with a chuckle, 'For fear of incriminating myself.'

It works; he laughs out loud. 'You're incriminated enough. Your face speaks louder than words.'

'Sorry. I remember what it's like to never be anything more than meat and muscle. I don't want to do that to you.'

'You remember ... as in it doesn't happen anymore? I find that hard to believe.'

I smile at his compliment but I answer his question. 'I know that it happens, why it happens and I avoid it. The ice queen thing works well. Plus, now I work with kids and that's easier.'

'What do you do?'

'I train kids, talented kids regardless of socio-economic standing.'

'Does that mean you train kids for free?'

'Some, yes. Others pay. Some are on scholarship-type programs.'

We walk and talk about athletics, funding, and life. Deep conversations for a 'first date'. However, the longer I'm with Cooper, the less it feels like a date. It's friends, talking and enjoying it. We aren't touching, we're walking together in synchronous movements and I'm happy. His company is fun, sexy and I'm more alive than I've felt for a long time.

We emerge from the silence of the rainforest to the pounding swish of surf and sand. The night air swirls, kissing my skin until goosebumps appear. I rub my hands up and down my arms and walk to the water's edge. I paddle, ankle deep, heading along the beach, kicking at the waves that ripple in. The sea's warmer than the breeze.

I ask him about football and we end up discussing the demands of our careers; the continuous cycle of training, travel and competing. He is totally absorbed by his football, to the detriment of having a life outside it.

'Don't you feel a need to balance football and life?'

'I couldn't find the perfect balance, so I gave up trying. I spend fifty weeks a year being a selfish prick who lives for football. I take two weeks a year to be human. Do you know what I mean?'

Nodding, I kick out at a wave, watching the green sparkles of the phospholuminescence dance across the water. 'You train hard and live for football. There's no time for anything else. Yeah, I remember what it's like.' I walk further, kicking at the water to watch the dazzle. I know how hard it is to train enough, eat right, sleep and somehow fit family, friendships and relationships in. It's almost impossible except with the perfect friend or partner.

'I'm interested in having some fun while I'm here.' Cooper's words send shivers of anticipation through me. I need to be more than just one night of 'fun'. I've outgrown that. I want more. I'm not saying marriage but there are a heap of levels between the extremes.

Deliberately obtuse, I try for innocence. 'I thought we had fun today. Well, I did.'

'I did too. I'm thinking more along the lines of turning my dive buddy into a bed buddy.'

I stop walking and he does too, close behind me. He's not touching, except with his breath that slides beneath my right earlobe making my flesh throb. His warmth extends so it licks at the back of my knees, along my hamstrings, across the top of my shoulders.

'This is a no-pressure question,' he adds when the silence has been too long.

I don't reply but the sound of rushing air comes from my nose, a cross between a sniffle and a snort. Those large hands close over my shoulders and his thumbs rub against my shoulder blades.

'Sorry, I shouldn't have asked. I thought you might have been interested.'

'Oh, I am. You haven't read that wrong.' I'm caving in. Easily. With no fight. But I haven't spent years of training and discipline to be a pushover. 'I have some rules.' He nods sharply and I continue. 'I'm clean but there's no sex unless it's safe and consensual. Agreed?'

'Agreed. And for the record, I'm clean too.'

I face him. In the moonlight he looks ... divinely edible. I lean forward, ever so slowly. I could be caught in freeze-frame. My gaze locks onto his perfect lips. The top bows beautifully but it's his bottom lip that is truly sinful. Pillow-plump, it beckons and calls. I sink towards him and after an agonising wait my lips touch his. I pause, resting my flesh against his for a second, savouring the sweet tingle of the initial caress. There's the momentary jolt of energy shifting between us as I press. This is followed by heaven as I sink into pillowy softness. His lips catch and hold mine. His hands circle my arms, warmth seeps in. I step closer, my body overshadowed by him, my feet tucked between his, while our kiss deepens.

There's the sharp sting of stubble against my mouth as we move. The kiss turns more demanding. No longer content to lounge in the softness, our lips fight for supremacy and submission. His press against mine, asking them to open but I'm demanding the same. We're both asking, neither answering, the tension mounts. We prod and press against each other until, on some unheard command, tension snaps. My mouth opens to him and his to mine.

He tastes of seafood, freshness, and salt. He's the wickedest dessert and I can't devour him quickly enough, nor have enough.

His hands run across my body, skimming my hips, my waist. My breath catches, waiting, hoping. His fingers sweep beneath my breasts and I exhale. My left hand curls into the musculature of his shoulder while my right slips around the strength of his neck and my fingers spear into the short hair at his nape, stretching upwards to cup his head. Our noses brush before our mouths open.

It's a quick break for breath and as our lips meet again, our tongues reach for each other's. They touch. Quivers rock me. His tongue is as strong as the rest of his body, curling around mine, teasing, pushing, stroking. He's dominating, pushing forwards, then retreating when I don't submit. Both my hands move to his head, holding so I can plunder his mouth properly. My fingertips knead the back of his head as our tongues twist and tangle. He cups his hands beneath my breasts and squeezes. I jump and pull away from the kiss, gasping, my breasts throbbing. I suck in air, hoping the lust-filled angst will pass. My nipples are standing out, so tight they could be torn from me by a passing gust.

Allowing me only a couple of gasps, he steps towards me and his palms immediately claim my breasts again. Through the fabric of my dress, he holds and weighs them, squeezes and slowly releases then squeezes again; slow exquisite torture. I want his thumbs on my nipples, or his mouth, but he only squeezes, watching as if he knows what it's doing to me. When he doesn't do anything more, I push at his upper arms but it's useless, they're rock solid muscle and I doubt he even notices my touch.

'What do you want, Samantha?' His voice is low, pitched against my ear as he leans towards me.

'My nipples ... please, my nipples.' I'm breathless. My words come out in gasps, begging.

'I can see them. They're pointed right at me, pushing through your dress. I bet they're rubbing against your bra right now.' And they are. *Bloody tease.* They're abrading against lace that was once soft and delicate but is now barbed wire.

'What do you want me to do with them, Samantha?'

'Touch them,' I manage to choke out. I can hardly think. All I want is the ache to go away, or stay and get better, or something.

He brushes his thumbs against both tips, together, in a sweep that leaves them aching more than before he touched them. My groan elicits his cute crooked grin. It makes my knees weaken but gives me the sense to say, 'Free them, suck them, taste them. Please.'

He releases his stranglehold on my breasts almost before I finish speaking. He unzips my dress and it falls to a puddle around my feet. His hands are at my bra clasp. He fumbles and I almost scream with need and then one clasp, two, three. He's deliberately making this tortuous. His eyes are dark but shining with laughter, or maybe the moonlight's encouraging my imagination. Finally my breasts tumble from their prison. Cool air makes me start and then his hands close across the middle of each breast, covering the nipple with the heat of his palm. Arching my back, I press deeper into his hands. For a few moments, it's heaven, and then he pulls away. A groan fills the air, followed by a deep chuckle. 'Why did I think you weren't interested?'

My growl only makes him chuckle more.

He cups my right breast in his hand, fingers closing on the nipple, tweaking and rolling it in his solid fingers. My head drops back, eyes rolling to the heavens as he plays. And before I can sigh my satisfaction, he closes his mouth on my left nipple. *Oh, God, yes.* Warm, wet, wonderful. I sigh and groan in one sound. My hand curves against the side of his face, thumb brushing his cheekbone, the edge of his eye, the curve of his ear. Fingers thread into his hair, massaging his scalp. My other hand is on his arm of steel, curling around muscles bunched tight and loosening as he moves.

Holy hell. I'm meant to be seducing him so I'm more than some chick who puts out on day one. Hundreds of girls must fall for him. My competitive edge is honed sharp. I have to be better than every single one of them. I need a point of difference, and the point cannot be the nipples he's feasting on.

My hands skim down his chest, stomach and dart over his hips. Hanging onto his hip bones, my thumbs brace either side of his cock, then rub simultaneously along the shorts-covered length.

His mouth pulls away from my breast. 'Fuck, yes.' His voice is a rumble slightly louder than the surf.

The fingers of my right hand close around his cock while my left hand splays against his chest. A deep fluttering develops in my lower belly. I take a big gulp before I can speak. 'Let me guess, Coop, you'd like the bed buddies to start right away?' I give a flirty grin.

'Hell yeah.'

'Not going to happen.'

He chuckles and leans in to capture my lips. I let them be caught, soaking up the fresh taste of him, leaning into his solid chest, stroking his strengthening cock. All the while, I keep a little bit of myself back, holding tightly to the tiniest shred of immune-to-caring-about-football-hunk.

I ease my hold on his cock as the kiss lessens. Moving back from him gently until he releases my lips.

'Ever had a girl walk away from you?' I make sure my words are light, almost a jest, and the smile on my face is fun and flirty.

He shakes his head. 'Nope. I've pushed plenty away but once it's on, it's on.'

I nod. 'And no frigging wonder. You're almost impossible to walk away from.' I wait long enough for our gazes to meet, lock and darken. As I think he's moving to capture me again, I grab my clothes, spin and dance a few steps down the beach out of reach.

A frown mars his face for a second and then his eyes widen. A low sound rumbles from his chest and expels as a desperately whispered, 'No.'

I grin evilly and dance a little further down the beach. 'Oh, yes. I'm the evil triathlete who knows how much better things are when you have to wait. And you, Cooper, are definitely going to be worth waiting for.'

'How long?' It's no plea. It's the same question he'd give a trainer who asks him to run further. I would have preferred him to argue or beg so my ego felt better, but I'd have despised him if he did.

I shrug and sneak close enough to run my fingertips along his forearm. 'No fixed term. I thought I'd see how long we can last. Doesn't that sound like more fun?'

As I dart away, I'm unable to decipher his growl, but since I'm not crash-tackled to the sand I can only assume he believes in fun.

Chapter 3

Dawn finally breaks on my restless night. I'm up and running from my thoughts. A hard run always pulls me into line, although today, I doubt that's possible since I've crossed into Cooper-crazy territory.

Malabar Hill is one of the steeper climbs on the island and not far from where I'm staying. I run towards that. I need pain to focus. If I can reach the top running, then my mind will quieten as every scrap of energy will be needed by my body, not my brain.

The slope has me slowing to a jog about three-quarters of the way up. It's vicious and I don't generally run on hills this big with this steep a gradient. My calves burn and thighs tense. My heart rate's pounding and my breath is coming in gasps. It's freaking hard work. Footfalls sound behind me, moving closer. Someone's gaining on me? That makes no sense. Lord, they must be fit to make that much ground on me. I'm not a useless runner ... but it is a big hill.

I up my pace to a fast jog. They aren't going to pass me. Air burns my throat before it fills my lungs. My thighs scream, calves knot in agonising spasms. I push through the pain.

Whoever is behind me is still closing in, and I'm pushing myself to breaking. Who the hell can be catching me? My back prickles, goosebumps rippling along my spine and across my shoulders.

'Morning, Sam.'

Cooper.

Of course.

With muscles like that, he'd need to hone them somehow. He doesn't even sound puffed.

I gather a breath and put everything I have into sounding normal. 'Good morning, Cooper. Lovely day.' I fail. My words spurt out between gasps.

'See you on the dive.' He continues running up the hill as if he's on the flat.

I follow his progress. Holy shit, he's fit. His calves are knotted tight, perfectly delineated. Thighs, deliciously defined, pump hard as they bunch rhythmically. He's shirtless and his back ripples from his neck to the top of his shorts. Running shorts as skin-hugging as his Speedos display a butt so tight it causes the breath to jam in my throat. Choking, I halt. I drop my head down towards my knees, and try to catch air. He's gone from view.

I could know what those muscles felt like if I wasn't so damn competitive. I could have had him last night. Licked every dip and swell. Feasted.

I fan my hand in front of my face and blink a thousand times. I hope to hell I haven't missed my chance.

I hadn't imagined him running past me. But I should have. I should have known he'd train hard to keep that shape, even if he is being human for a fortnight.

No human should be able to run up this hill like he just did.

I reach the top of the climb at a slow jog before heading back down, my thoughts somewhat quietened by my exertion. Cooper doesn't pass me again. I'm glad. I don't need all those lusty thoughts again.

When I return, time moves slowly. I wonder how far Cooper ran, if he's returned, if he's twisted an ankle or stretched a muscle. Stupid things. Things I have no right thinking about let alone worrying about. He's gotten under my skin. In a day. Too deep, too quickly.

I head to the lagoon beach to snorkel for an hour before the dive. The beach is deserted, just how I like it. I put my towel and keys and Cooper's washed towel and snorkelling gear on the sand beside the rocky point and head in. With my face in the water I'll look at fish and not keep twisting my neck, straining for a glimpse of Cooper.

The water's cool after the warmth I've generated. The lapping motion of the sea immediately calms me. Fish dart before my mask and sunlight streams through the water as if it's glass, highlighting rocks, weed, fish, shells, colours, movements. My mind stills and I lose myself in the majesty of the underwater world.

A brush against my foot sets my heart in my throat. 'Shark!' immediately springs to mind but in the second it takes for the word to form, I settle myself and think it's more likely seaweed touching me. I kick away a little, still entranced by the world below me.

Another brush and I turn. It's not seaweed but the brush of fingertips. Fingers belonging to the dimple-faced man I had momentarily forgotten. I tread water and remove my snorkel before speaking. 'Hey.'

'Hey, yourself. How did your jog go?'

My jog? The one I call a run? I smile instead of grimacing. 'Fine, thanks. Your run?'

'Good. Hard. Just what I needed. Much to see here?'

I shrug. 'Nothing like Neds but there are lots of little fish.'

'Mind if I join you?'

I enjoy being asked even if there's zero chance of my rejection. 'Not at all.'

'Thanks for washing my gear, Sam. I owe you.'

We snorkel for another 40 minutes and even with him beside me, it's relaxing. He taps my arm and points to his watch. Time to dive. We make our way back to the beach.

Walking out of the water, he shakes himself and my eyes are drawn. How can they not be? He's magnificent. The nerves in my body, soothed in the salt water, are again frayed. They shoot sparks through synapses at random moments making my whole body tense, jumpy and ready to scream in frustration. I need to be back in the calming sea. Or, *fuck,* plastered across those muscles.

Wordlessly I grab my towel and blot it against my face, hoping to hide the lustful gaze, the blush of need. When I've regained a semblance of control, I knot the towel around myself and we make our way to the dive shop.

I like our unspoken communication. We grab dive gear, attach buoyancy control devices to air cylinders, regulators are fitted and tested. We suit up, grab fins and head to the boat. Stowing gear, we work like a long-standing team. Then side-by-side against the railing we listen to the dive brief.

It's our second dive together but it might as well have been our hundredth. I know how it's going to go, what we both want to see, and it's an unusual heady feeling.

The boat starts and we make our way to the site.

I think I know what we're wanting, but it pays to check. 'So, our plan for the dive is?'

He turns towards me and his tongue does a quick sweep across his lips. My eyes follow greedily before

I consciously pull my gaze away and settle on the horizon.

'Don't drown.'

I quickly snap my head back to stare at him, mouth open. He grins and his fingers press against my lower jaw.

'Sorry, I couldn't resist.' He's not sorry at all. 'I'm happy to drop down, see what's there and poke around. How about you?'

'That suits me fine.'

'Have you dived this site before?' I nod and he asks, 'Do you want to head away from the drop zone and explore new territory?'

'It's new every time I dive. I reckon we see where everyone else goes and find somewhere quiet.' And I hope that doesn't sound as suggestive as it does to my ears. I hope there's no blush creeping up my face.

There must be. That little crooked smile appears, the one that presses a pseudo-dimple into the right side of his mouth, before he says, 'Sounds perfect to me.'

I'm in so much trouble. There's no way I should have made him wait. It's killing me. Somehow I need to get this under control.

The water is perfect. The dive, incredible. My buddy, the best I've dived with. He's cautious but fun. He enjoys touching, not just sea life but me too. My arm, my hand, a brush against my leg. I always know where he is and while it's a libido-nuisance, I'm reassured. He smiles, talks underwater, and uses hand signals so I know he's enjoying the dive. And it's sometimes in stereo, each of us making the same noise as we see something spectacular—lion fish, a school of kingfish, an eel, reef sharks, a school of angelfish.

The underwater world cools my heated thoughts. The wetsuit protects me from shivers and quivers, prickles and goosebumps. When he touches me, I turn to see what he's found, not to see if he's ready to fuck.

An hour later, we're packed up and gear's washed down. 'Lunch?' he asks with his head cocked to the side, as if he expects me to reject the offer.

'Lunch would be great.' We smile as if we're talking about more than food. Everything has sexual connotations now. The air between us sizzles with sexual tension.

'I'll go grab it. Be back soon.' Cooper darts off before I can respond. I sit on the beach and wait for him. The lazy lapping of the ocean and the warmth of the sun calms me to an almost doze.

Moments later, the smell of freshly grilled fish and lemon assaults me. A box of food drifts in front of my face and settles before me. Cooper's bulky shoulder is above mine and near my face as he leans over. I turn and nip at the tense muscle, perfectly positioned at lip height.

After a low rumble response, I ask, 'Did you pre-order?'

Grinning, he lays out the food. 'Yeah. I didn't want to be starving like yesterday.'

I can't help but chuckle. He has enough here to hold back any hunger—for food, at least.

Once the mountain of food is spread out and he's given me a bowl, he sits next to me. His arm brushes mine as he reaches for lunch. I want my wetsuit back on. How much longer will I be able to hold out? He's not exactly playing fair ... but I should have expected that.

'Smells great, doesn't it?' Before I can answer, he's broken off a chunk of fish and slipped it between his lips. I almost groan watching the white fish against his pink lips, the lemon juice shining across the rise of his lower lip before slipping to the corner of his mouth. He swallows, licks his fingers and his tongue flicks against his lips wiping them clean.

'Eat,' he commands, and I drag my gaze from his mouth to the food. 'You'll need your energy.' His eyes sparkle, and paired with his wicked grin, my chest tightens as I imagine all manner of mischief I'll need energy for. My heart speeds and my brain stalls before he nudges me and points at the food.

Grilled fish and salad is perfect. I break up fillets and mix it in my bowl with salad while Cooper watches. 'Good idea.' Together we break up the rest, mixing it through the salad. Our white plastic forks rhythmically dip in and out of the bowls. I have my fill and sit back while he continues. I keep my eyes on anything but him. The water is a distraction. The little island further out. The occasional white cloud drifting by. They aren't great deterrents to watching him eat. For once, I wish seagulls were annoying me, but there are none. I could devour him now. Damn my competitive spirit.

When he finishes eating, he gives a full blast of the crooked, dimple-producing smile. Everything inside me twists and flips. A dramatic twist and roll. Fully blown lust spears.

If only I'd followed through last night, we'd be sated ... and he'd be bored. I have to believe in my decision no matter how it hurts.

'Did you make plans for this arvo?' he asks as he returns from throwing away the rubbish.

'No.'

'Can you handle another hill walk?'

'Sure. Although I won't be able to match your pace.' I hate admitting that.

He laughs. 'I wasn't expecting you to. I don't need another run. I found a great view this morning. I want to take some photos this afternoon while the sun is behind me.'

'You take photos?' This surprises me. It's a very non-physical pastime for such an active man.

'I'm not a total meathead, you know.' He grins but there's a touch of defensiveness behind the words. He's no fool. His diving showed me that and I wonder why he doesn't do underwater photography too.

We split up to grab our gear before meeting up to walk to the northern end of the island and climb Mount Eliza. On the flat walk to the north, we jog most of the way. It's quiet with no one else around. I work hard not to slow him down. Sometimes he's next to me. When he gets ahead of me, I stretch the jog to a run to keep up. It's not easy competing with him but it's a lot of fun. He's pushing me but he won't break me. I've spent years developing my stamina and mental strength. Besides, the climb is not as steep as this morning's.

As we come to a small level section before what looks like the last part of the hill, Cooper pulls off the track. 'The rest of the track's closed to protect the breeding red-tailed tropicbirds and sooty terns.'

'Are you serious?'

'There's a sign just up ahead. Go, check it out, I'll grab some photos.'

He's not going to make up something like that but I jog further up the track and see the sign for myself before coming back. It's a shame we can't go on. The view of the lagoon and the southern end of the island must be even more brilliant at the top than it is here. 'No wonder you wanted these photos. The weather is perfect. Look at the colours in the lagoon.' The reefs, deep holes and shallow sandy spots are depicted in all shades of blue and green. Turquoise, aqua, bright emerald. With the azure sky and the green-grey mountains as a backdrop, it's glorious.

Cooper takes a few shots. 'It was nice this morning but the afternoon sun brings out the colours and makes it spectacular.'

'Give me your camera and I'll take one of you with the view.' It's the only thing that will make the view any better. I take his photo. A thought strikes me. 'Did you run right across the island this morning?'

He looks a bit sheepish. 'Not right across. I just did this end.'

I'm speechless. He's on holidays and doing that much work? I wonder what he's like when he's really focussed on football.

He must know I'm questioning his sanity as he tries justifying himself before admitting the truth. 'Okay, so I had trouble sleeping.' There's no response to that except my laughter.

Cooper swats me. 'How about a picture of you, Sammy?'

I hand him back his camera. 'Will I get to see them?'

He grins. 'Sure. I'll email them to you. Just give me your addy.'

He snaps a photo of me and then comes beside me, slides one arm around my waist, the other outstretched holding the camera. He's taking a photo of us both?

Laughing, I turn to face him and our lips touch then lock tight. The kiss sucks the breath from me. I wrap my body against his, drawing closer. He holds my head and hours of sexual frustration pour into the kiss. Mouths open as we feast on each other. Tongues touch tentatively before slipping, sliding over each other and tangling around.

He cradles my head while his fingers stroke and massage my scalp. My hands roam his back, his sides, his butt. Muscles move tantalisingly beneath my fingertips. He grinds his hips against mine as the kiss heats further.

Silently cursing my stupidity at pulling away from him last night, I'm ready to fuck him now. Wet and willing. Before I can reach between us to pull his cock free, a cool draught flutters over me and warm palms capture my buttocks. My naked buttocks. Cooper's slid my shorts and bikini bottoms down to my knees.

'*You* might want me to wait but I need to make you come.'

Shit. His words almost have me doing that even before he's touched me. Pressing my back against the rocks behind us, he drops to his knees.

'Oh, Sam. You're bare.' From the rawness of his voice I know he's pleased. Before I can respond, he pushes his head between my thighs.

I grab fistfuls of his thick brown hair. 'Fuck. Cooper.'

I can't quite hear what he says before his tongue obliterates my sanity but it sounds like, 'That's it exactly.'

I'm half-clothed, exposed, outdoors, in public, and I couldn't give a damn. Excitement thrums. Cooper's hot breath is on me. His tongue licks against my thighs, my labia and into my soaking slit. Arching in complete ecstasy, I rock my hips against his face. I've been on the point of burning, aching arousal, one-touch-before orgasm since seeing him and now I'm going to burn into oblivion.

His tongue slides towards my clit. Every cell tenses. As soon as he touches it, I'll be gone. Fireworks in space. And he's close. So close. The wet heat is right there, just beside where I need it, and not getting any closer.

'Cooper.' My cry is one of torment, agony, desperation. He laughs and heated air is expelled across my clit.

Oh, oh, oh.

No. It's not enough. I'm going to die. My back rasps against the jagged edges of the rocks. My eyes scrunch tight, my face screws up holding in my anguish.

And then his tongue flicks. Once. Softly.

My body vibrates with need. *Please. Oh please. Oh please.* Then a harder slick rolls across my clit, deep and strong.

'Yes.' My cry is loud enough to be heard all over the island and I don't care. He laps across my clit faster and faster as he elicits the first orgasm from me and keeps me soaring.

His tongue plunges into my cunt and I imagine his mouth covered in my come. And I want to taste him. I want to taste me on him. He tongue-fucks me until every part of me collapses. I slide down the rock wall as Cooper catches me. I can focus on only one thing—kissing Cooper and tasting. I cling to him and devour his lips, while his fingers slide inside me.

Heady flavours fill me. The rich earthy taste of sex. Part musk, part salt, part Cooper. His lips are as hungry as mine. It's a kiss like last night's; demanding and asking, pushing and retreating, dominating and questioning. Neither of us giving control, but neither of us taking it from the other, making it an erotic compromise.

His fingers move inside me. Pushing, stretching, keeping me balanced on the orgasm precipice again.

While I'm caught in Cooper's spell, nothing infiltrates. Not the silence, not the scents, nor the people coming up the track and trying to get past.

Cooper pulls back, breaking the kiss. He holds me upright with hands digging into my hips. I pant against his chest and try to focus on reality. The reality of a broken kiss, an empty cunt, an orgasm lost and a world that is no longer silent. Cooper moves in front, smothering me.

'Sorry, mate.' The stranger's voice hits like a freak wave. I freeze. Cooper holds me close, protecting me while three older men pass. I try to wriggle free when they've gone but Cooper keeps hold, hissing at me to be still.

Within moments, the men return, passing us again. 'Closed for mating season,' one of them mutters as they head back down the track.

The guy's words and our predicament are too funny. I try to hold in my chuckles but they burst from me as inelegant snorts, made worse as I try to keep quiet. 'We should've been on the other side of the sign.' My eyes water and my nose runs as I propel gusts of giggles.

Cooper's laughing with me. We're like teenagers caught snogging by their mates.

'Sorry. I didn't hear them coming.' Cooper brushes his fingers across my face before reaching down to drag up my shorts and swimmers. I can only hope my naked state wasn't noticed by the men.

'Hell, it's certainly not your fault.' I pause to give Cooper the evil eye with a grin. 'Although, you did start it.'

'If you hadn't run away last night we wouldn't be so het up we'd need interrupting.'

I smirk. 'But if I didn't run away, I'd be forgettable. Just another notch in your bedpost or goalpost or whatever you use.'

He pulls my arm to his side and stares intently at me. The air thickens. My heart thunders. I dare not pre-empt what he might say and waiting lasts a lifetime.

Ever so slowly a smile lights his eyes. 'I won't be able to forget this.' He pauses a beat. 'And I doubt I'll be able to forget you.' Another pause. 'A woman who can almost keep up with me.'

Not a romantic declaration but enough to make my heart swell and my ego soar. And just to make sure he remembers me, I tug my hand free and take off at a sprint, shouting behind me, 'Race you to the bottom of the hill.' If I can keep him behind me on the trail, I have a hope of winning.

***

Our night dive follows the pattern of our other dives, except we have a fluoro stick attached to our tank and a torch in our hands. And there's a different feeling on a night dive. It's more isolating than usual—you can't see very far so it's like you're exploring an aquarium, not the ocean. Sometimes, if I think about how vast and dark it is, I freak myself out. To control this, I think only as far as my torch beam. Who wants to know what lurks beyond the light?

When we reach the bottom and check with each other, we have a third member of our party. A metre long reef shark is beside me, like a stray puppy that won't leave. I reach out to brush against its side and it bends around my touch rather than swimming away. I look at Cooper who shrugs. I'm okay with a shark if Cooper is. These ones don't bite. Luckily Cooper's okay with it too because I have no idea how to lose a shark when it's taken a liking to you.

Our party of three sets off to explore the lagoon by night. We swim over rocks we've seen in daylight but by night they're eerier, larger, and the inhabitants different.

I have a guard either side of me. Cooper's body is warmer by night, drawing me closer to him. With his fluoro stick I'd see him even if I moved metres away and I make myself do that. Pathetic that I'm hanging off him like a limpet. He'll think I'm afraid of the dark, or the shark, when all I need is his warmth. *Okay, I want more than his warmth, but not underwater.*

The longer I'm near him, the more I want from him and that's a foreign feeling. I'm independent. Happy to live in a disposable society. Men are easy come, easy go. Usually. I doubt I'll forget Cooper.

The stray-puppy shark keeps just out of easy petting distance but never leaves my side. I reach out and graze my fingertips across the edge of its pectoral fin. The sandpapery feel isn't as pronounced *** underwater with my pruney fingers.

Cooper shakes his head and mimes. One hand reaches out and the other snaps over it. I chuckle and shake my head. I'm pretty sure the shark isn't going to bite me. Reef sharks aren't aggressive, and I'm not grabbing at it or annoying it.

Tonight's dive doesn't relax me like the others have. I'm keyed up with need. I want Cooper. I want to finish what we started this afternoon. I want to touch him, have him inside me, bring him to his knees.

Before ascending at the end of the dive, I tap my fingers over the back of Cooper's hand to catch his attention. Kneeling on the sand at the bottom of the sea, I suck a deep breath for courage and stick the torch beneath my chin. Two hands are needed. I hope that by saying this underwater, it's fun. Intimate. Different. Something to remember. Besides, I can't get into too much immediate trouble with two wetsuits between us.

Cooper kneels in front of me, which is lucky because he'll probably fall over when he gets my message.

Holding my fingers tight in the torchlight, I make a very direct point at him. Then I point at me. He's watching. That dark brown gaze not leaving my hands in case he misses the message. I like this about him; he pays attention.

I make a circle with the fingers and thumb of my left hand. Not the okay signal; all my fingers are tucked into a cylinder. With my right hand, I make a gun-shape with my index and middle fingers pointed as the gun. Tucking in my thumb, I take the gun shape, and keeping my gaze on his face, insert my fingers into the circle of my left hand. Insert and remove, insert and remove. I pump my hand faster until I see his eyes widen. I stop, my hands drop to my side. When there's no response from Cooper, my heart stalls in my chest. Surely he understands? How completely embarrassing. I give an okay signal hoping he's worked it out. If I could hold my breath I'd be doing that but you aren't supposed to hold your breath while scuba diving. I don't suppose those rules apply when you've made a total twat of yourself.

Finally, a burst of bubbles explode around Cooper's face. Thank goodness. I thought for a moment I had an epic crash and burn. He's lost in fizz. The shark swims above Cooper's head and luxuriates in the mass of bubbles. I imagine them popping and tickling its stomach. Maybe that's why it's followed us, looking for a mini spa bath.

Cooper picks up my hand and nods his head. He gives an okay, then taking the regulator from his mouth, he presses his lips to the back of my hand and my insides become a mushy mess. I've found a knight underwater where his armour will rust.

He gives a pulse of air to his reg as he returns it to his mouth. The shark dances in more fizz. I chuckle, torn between watching the shark relishing the bubbles and drowning in Cooper's dark chocolate gaze.

We've used up a lot of air, so we make our way back to the boat, leaving our pet shark in bubble bliss.

The packing up is a blur. I work by rote, glad that I've done this so many times I can do it without thought. Gear's washed and stowed. Goodnights are finally said and we're walking back to town.

'Your place or mine?' Cooper's words sound like they're gritted between his teeth. We've hardly spoken since surfacing but these tell me all I need to know.

I hesitate and he sweeps my hand into his, leading me away from the dive shack. 'Mine's closer.' It's a growl.

His pace picks up to a fast walk. My lips twitch as I fight back a grin. I shake my hand free and he glares. I smirk. 'Race you.' I take off running, as fast as I can with a mask and snorkel flapping at my side and a wet towel catching against my legs. I need to stop racing him. It's taking all I have to beat him and I'm not sure he's putting in one hundred per cent. It's fun, though, the challenge he poses.

We pull up in front of his abode, me lightly panting and he hardly puffing. Droplets run down my back, between my breasts, and down my arms. A tiny pool lingers behind each knee, not yet running down my calf. I doubt Cooper's broken a sweat. *Lord he's fit.*

The key's in the door and we're inside. The door closes with a snap behind me. *Holy hell. Luxury living.* I'd like to drop my gear here but the wood floors are beautifully polished and a wet towel lying there all night would ruin them, surely. *Idiot. Who cares?* But I do. With this much luxury, how can you not?

My hands beg to splay against Cooper's back but I can't. If I touch him, I won't give a hoot about the wood floors. Cooper heads straight to the bathroom. He drops his mask and snorkel into the sink and mine follow. I drop my towel to the tiled floor and reach for the strap on my swimmers.

'No.' The growl stops me. His hand snags the strap of my swimmers. Heat bursts through me, inciting a riot of action inside and outside. Everything inside tingles, churns, screams and writhes. Outside I'm faking calm, making deliberate sweeps across his flesh. Fingertips against his nipples. Thumb into navel. Flat hands following the band of muscle over his hips. My fingers hook into the waistband of his swimmers and shimmy them down, feeling his cock rise against me. I shudder. A groan escapes my lips before I close my hands on the naked globes of his butt.

And all this time, he's kept his hands on my shoulders. His head thrown back and eyes closed.

This mass of glorious muscle is mine to explore, to taste, to tease. I take a small step backwards and drag my hands from his arse to his hips and inch them towards his cock. It bobs, semi-erect, as if waiting for my touch. I kneel on the bathroom floor and trace my fingertip along the length. It twitches continuously, silently begging for a firmer touch. It's different to those I've seen before. A swathe of skin surrounds it. The men I've partnered have been circumcised and I don't know if I have to treat this differently.

He must feel the hesitation of my touch because he looks down, eyes almost hidden by heavy lids. 'Yes?'

'You're...' I stop, struggling to justify my lack of knowledge. 'It's not that I'm inexperienced. I've just not been with men, men who, you know, are intact.' *Seriously classy, Sam.*

'Most men are skinned, I know, but it's changing.' There's an almost defensive air to his voice but he doesn't look like he's embarrassed, for himself or for me. He looks like he's challenging me.

His word choice makes me shudder. 'That's awful. Skinned?'

'Well, that's what happens, isn't it?'

I shrug, not wanting to have a philosophical discussion on circumcision, but eager to touch his unskinned cock correctly. 'So, um, do I do anything different?' Geez, I sound like a bloody virgin. But I don't know how to handle the extra skin and surely it's better to ask and learn.

Cooper laughs and closes his fist on his cock. 'It the same as all the others, but you get to unwrap the present.' He slides his hand towards his body, skin moving to expose the head of his cock. My mouth waters. 'Just push the skin back. It moves freely. It's no different, really, just an extra flap of skin.' His hands move to his hips, white knuckles appear.

'It is different. It's beautiful.' I touch my fingers to the flesh-covered head of his cock and squeeze slightly. His cock is hard beneath and peeks through the foreskin. It is like peeking into a present. I adjust so my eyes are level with the gift. I curl my fingers around the head of his cock and slide them towards his body. The head juts out of the flesh.

'Oh, Lord.' My voice holds reverence and awe. There's something god-like about this man. And to be untouched, unmarked, how Nature honed him, does incredible things to my brain. In a rush of purely animal instinct, I lean down and brush the flat of my tongue across the tip of his penis. The salty taste of the ocean and Cooper fills my mouth. My tongue lingers a few moments before lifting away.

'Fuck, that's good.' His hands grasp the doorway and the sink. Legs apart, open and granting me access to his body. That's one thing sportsmen have over other men—the ability to be confident naked, to display their body proudly and to accept admiration.

I close my lips around his cock head and suck him inside, not too deep, teasing. His cock fills my senses—the velvet flesh, the steely strength, the salty tang. Nothing has felt so good. Nothing has tasted so good. And nothing tempts me as much as Cooper.

I swirl my tongue across the tip, skirting around the edge before flicking at the slit.

'Suck it, Sam. Take me inside your mouth.'

Cooper's words make me grin. I press my lips to the top of his cock before sitting back on my heels. Catching his gaze has me smirking even more.

The frown marring his forehead is deeply etched, his eyes have narrowed and his lips thinned. 'You are totally unbelievable, incredibly cruel—'

'And you love every second of it.' I grin, hoping that I'm not pushing too far.

He holds his cock in his huge hand and strokes it slowly, slipping the skin back and forth until my gaze drops from his face down his chest to his groin. I'm watching nothing but his fist, waiting for the head of his cock to show.

With no conscious thought I lean forward, my hand closing over his fist, and lap at his cock as it peeks through. His other hand slips behind my head, moulding to the back of my skull as his fingertips massage. My mouth drops open and he feeds his cock slowly inside, my tongue lapping at each newly introduced millimetre of flesh. His fist uncurls and I move my hand to the base of his cock, holding it tight as he had been.

'Fuck, Sam. That's good.' It's nice of him to give encouragement but it isn't true. I haven't got to the good part yet.

Mouth open, head back, I take his cock deep, lips closing tight near the base. I pull my head backwards, inching slowly off him until the head is the only portion inside. With a swirl of my tongue, I push back down, speeding up the movements until his cock is fucking my mouth decadently. Saliva fills my mouth, lubricating each thrust.

Big firm hands close on my shoulders, pulling me away from his cock and up from the bathroom floor.

'What?' My question is more a harsh accusation.

'The bathroom tiles are cold. I don't want you hurting your knees.'

Laughing, I pinch his chin. 'You're a control freak who doesn't want to come too quickly.'

The noise he makes is more a scoff than a chuckle. He picks me up and carts me to the bed; a huge expanse of mattress smothered with pillows.

Chapter 4

While carting me to the bed, he unties my bikini top and as he throws me onto the doona, the bottoms slip off and the top drops away. 'Nifty nakedness trick,' I say with a chuckle.

He stares, his gaze without waver. My laughter vanishes. Lust unfurls through my body and flames. He prowls on hands and knees until he's beside me, and then his teeth nip my earlobe. My head rolls back, supported by clouds of pillows and he feasts on my neck, ear and shoulder. The softness of his lips, the warmth of his breath, the wet flick of his tongue makes me languid. The sharp nip of teeth on the soft flesh beneath my ear sends sparks through me, each nerve waiting, wanting.

He tugs me while he sprawls, until his body shapes around mine, his front plastered against my rear. I wrap a foot behind his leg and rub the top along the back of his calf. Then using my leg as leverage, I heave myself on top. He twists, grabs at me, and I wrestle back until we're sprawling across each other, laughing like five-year-olds.

A bubbly high fills my bloodstream, like I've knocked back a few glasses of champagne. My heart sprouts wings that are flapping hard. Muscles writhe, skin against skin. I'm rolling with a naked, gorgeous, muscled hunk of manhood who's caring, kind, and fun. He's making a huge impression on me. And my impression on him? I'm a 38-year-old retired athlete who's never seen an unskinned man and who laughs like a child in the middle of sex. Not so good ... but memorable.

Ending up on top, I press a thousand kisses on his body. Slow, wet, sucking kisses. Exploring each muscular bump and dip. Tiny nips, followed by a darting tongue. A slow lap. Lips pressed tightly around nipples, sucking. While I'm lost in the shape of his chest, luxuriating in the taste of him, he grabs me and flips me onto my back.

Holding my ankles, he bends my knees and places my feet flat against his chest. He leans down and runs his tongue from my left instep up to the inside of my leg. My breath is held. His mouth trails over the swell of my calf, into the dip at the inside of my knee. I expect him to traverse my thigh and suckle me when he nips the swell at the junction of thigh and knee.

'Yow!' I arch and my body jerks. My reaction is intense. My cunt fills. Shivers flood me. My flesh runs with electricity.

He licks at the nipped flesh. With a huge grin, he lets my legs go and straddles me on the bed. 'Don't you like being bitten?'

I trace the edge of his lower lip with my fingertip. 'I didn't dislike it. The shock made me jump.'

'So I could bite you again?' His words are laced with suggestion.

'Maybe.' I grin.

Cooper, kneeling, runs his hands down the outer edge of my body before grasping my hips and leaning onto them. He's heavy but most of his weight must be on his knees. His gaze drills me. 'What else can I do?'

I laugh. 'I signed up for sex, not 20 questions.'

After a brief grimace and a little frown, he says, 'I don't want to do something and end up on a television program because of it.'

Visions of news coverage about football players being lambasted for sexual exploits pop into my mind. I haven't paid a lot of attention but even I'm aware of what he's talking about. 'I'm not a media girl. For me, what happens in the bedroom stays in the bedroom.'

'And if we're not in the bedroom?' A wicked gleam comes to his eye.

I laugh before slipping my hands over his jaw and cheeks. 'Whatever happens between us, stays between us. I promise. So long as we have condoms and consent, I'll be fine.'

He slides against my body until his lips meet mine. His weight settles on me but again, mostly on the bed. His lips nibble so lightly it's almost as if they're not moving.

I open my mouth but instead of accepting my invitation and pushing the kiss further, Cooper pulls back and drops tiny butterfly kisses along my nose to my forehead.

Our gazes meet, lock and challenge before our mouths follow the same course. There's nothing gentle about this coming together. The merge is desperate and wild. He fills me, his tongue against mine, against my lips, in my mouth. His scent in my nostrils. I can't get enough. I writhe beneath his weight, trying to arch and rub my nipples against his chest, feel his cock against my thighs, but I'm as good as pinned down. It's exhilarating.

My breathing accelerates as the excitement grows. My body is aching for his touch but the kiss is so intoxicating that I never want it to end. I meet every one of his tongue's thrusts and parries with my own.

Great kissing means great chemistry. You can't kiss someone for any length of time if there isn't good chemistry between you.

When our kiss heats to boiling, he tones it down to deep motionless kisses. He nibbles across then slowly sucks on my bottom lip until I'm aching. Then we kiss again, building up, and he slows. All the while his gaze hardly leaves mine.

When I'm completely kiss-drunk and can't think of my own name, he lifts and cool air slips between us.

He holds himself up on his hands and knees and stares at me, panting.

'Wow.' I breathe the word but he hears, or reads my lips.

'Hot, huh?' He gives his cute one-dimple smile, which has my stomach lurching happily.

After a few moments of staring mindlessly, my senses come back to me. Cooper comes into focus, his eyes sparkling. His breath is a sweet whisper across my lips. His body a warm blanket over me. My mind kicks into gear. 'It'll be hotter if you let me on top.' Grinning what I hope is a tempting smile, I squirm beneath him.

'Why's that hotter than having you trapped beneath me?' His hips thrust against mine, emphasising words and punctuating his question, almost stalling my brain function.

I grin to make sure he knows I'm joking. 'I won't have to worry about you falling and squashing me.' He chuckles and I continue pushing my claim. 'You'd be able to use your hands on me instead of holding yourself up.' My body's desperate for his touch.

His lips twist and his eyebrow raises. 'And that's beneficial to me?'

'Oh, umm...' Damn, I can't think of any reason it would benefit him. *Oh, hang on.* 'If I'm on top, you'll get deeper penetration. That'll be better for you.'

'And you're telling me that won't be good for you?' His stomach-flipping grin causes mine to do just that.

'Oh, hey, mutually beneficial. Isn't that what we're looking for?'

He flips me faster than a blink. I'm now perched over him while his legs hang off the bed.

'I don't know what you're looking for,' he says, 'but I'm sick of talking. Condoms are in the top drawer. If you want to fuck, I was ready last night.'

I laugh, loudly, and reach for the top drawer. If I'm completely honest, I was ready the moment we surfaced on the first dive, before I even saw all those muscles.

His hands clasp my hips while I twist and reach for the drawer. This innocent touch makes my nipples tighten painfully. I want his hands on them, not my hips. But as he pointed out, it's not all about me and I've tormented him long enough, probably too long.

Grasping a condom, I wriggle to settle myself straddling his thighs. His cock stands tall, waiting as impatiently as its owner for my attention. My mouth moistens thinking about taking his cock inside but an impatient growl has my focus back on the condom.

I have the rubber mostly on when Cooper's hands slide from my hips to the inside of my thighs and his fingers slip against my slick labia. 'Oh, God, yes.' I finish with the condom even while my hands shake.

Before I can move, his finger slides inside me. My head drops back and a groan escapes. My fingers curl tightly around the base of his cock and I squirm, pushing downwards against his hand. 'Fuck me, Cooper.' In response, both his hands move to my hips.

His fingers still. When I look pointedly at him, he smirks. 'I thought you were going to do all the work.'

Chuckling, I position myself over his cock and angle the head towards me. Rocking my hips I feel the latex-covered cock head before pushing down for a perfect body invasion. Muscles stretch. It's heaven. He's large but not uncomfortably so. I take my time, feeling muscles work not only in my cunt as it stretches but in my thighs as I hold myself over him. I can't draw my gaze from his face. His head's thrown back as if he's holding tight to his need. The hard line of his jaw is tantalising. I want to bite that jaw and lick at the soft flesh beneath before sucking and biting my way down his neck.

I can't continue this slow invasion. I sink onto him, gasping from the sudden fullness.

Cooper sits up on an exhalation. His scrunched abdomen catches my attention before his lips close over my left nipple. Wet heat fills my mind, blinding my memory. I press my breast further into his mouth. It's bliss. And then his fingers capture my right nipple and it's a bliss I've never known. I lift my hips, his cock moves, pushing against inner walls. Waves of pleasure surge through me. He sucks, nibbles, bites, licks and breathes on my nipple. I squirm for all I'm worth, rocking my hips so his cock slides within.

I need to move. I need his cock thrusting into me. I can't stand this restricted movement. But I need him to suckle. I can't have both. 'Argh.' Frustration bursts from me. Cooper lifts his head, his fingers on both nipples now. Needing nothing more, my hips lift, rising and falling on his shaft, faster and faster. He tugs my nipples, they stretch away from my body further than they should. I thrust down, a guttural scream locked in my throat. He releases my nipples, clasps my hips and joins my rhythm.

I can't hold back. Arching, my lower body slamming against his, I cry out. Wave after wave of pleasure surges. My nipples buzz, sting, throb. A wave of cool air washes over them and my body convulses. Hips slam hard, my cunt tightens around Cooper's cock, walls contract, moisture explodes and I'm swamped. Colours, sound and waves of endorphins fill me. I've never buzzed like this. I'm on a plane above the earth, somewhere I can't think, can't move, can only feel.

A guttural 'Fuck,' fills the air and Cooper peaks with me. We're suspended. Gazes locked. Unable to move. The air between us alive and screaming.

The intensity weakens. Slowly, so slowly, we drift back to earth. My thighs grip his legs like a jockey suspended above a thoroughbred. A burning ache rips along my quads, forcing me to release Cooper's legs. I ease down so my knees are on the bed, holding my weight, but I'm still pinned by his cock.

I stretch out the knots in my back. Muscles soothed by orgasmic release move easily and make me happily languid. I hold myself upright although I'd like to sprawl across his chest.

'You're right,' Cooper says with slurring words. 'It was better for waiting.'

I grin. 'How do you know it wasn't going to be that good without waiting?'

He lifts my hips from him. The loss of the warmth and fullness sends a lance of disappointment through my chest. 'It's never that good first up.' He smiles and indicates the condom. 'I'll just get rid of this.'

I lie on my side, watching as he saunters into the bathroom. He has a bloody fantastic butt. Tight and round, it hollows at the base when he walks. Lord, I want to grab hold of him and fuck him again.

He heads back, a grin on his face as if he knows exactly what I'm thinking. 'I need a rest. Sorry, much as I've tried, I haven't been able to improve the stamina of my cock.'

I laugh. He knows he's a package any woman would drool over, yet he laughs about it. I love it.

'You rest, muscle-boy. I'm sure I'll be able to amuse myself for a while,' I leer.

He lies beside me. 'Just let me rest for a bit and I'll be all yours again. Up for round two.'

I trace my index finger across his hand and work my way along his arm and over his shoulder. I've never had the opportunity to study muscles this well-developed. I've always been with fit men, but none so heavily muscled. His biceps and triceps are like mini-mountains, even in semi-repose. The hills and valleys are more exciting than a Sunday run through the Adelaide hills. The muscles of his neck are thick and hard, an extension of his shoulders. Touring his chest is thrilling. The smooth dome across his pectorals is like a super-large version of his cock head, although nipples are tight dark nubs, not a single slit. I lick them the same as I would the slit, probing with the tip of my tongue. He moans softly, his eyes half-closed as he watches.

'I thought you were resting?'

He makes a tiny snort before speaking. 'You think I can rest with your fingers dancing around like that?'

'Do you want me to stop?'

'God, no. Just don't expect me to perform.' He gives a lazy smile full of self-satisfied confidence.

My left hand traces the musculature of his stomach. A six pack with more than six packed in. I let my fingers explore dips and hills, evenly spaced across the wide expanse. Each ripple receives my touch. Each groove the sweep of my thumb. And when my fingers have finished exploring, I take my tongue on the journey. Pockets of sweat strengthen the taste of Cooper. A stretch of warm, tight muscle and I slick across as if skating. His flesh is a feast for the famished. I can't slake my need.

Once his stomach is thoroughly examined, it's the perfect opportunity to move on. My fingers curl lightly around his semi-flaccid cock, and I stroke the loose flesh so it moves along the shaft freely. I slip the skin back from the head, holding it as I examine the smooth rounded top. Leaning forward I slide the flat of my tongue across the dome. With only a hint of latex, a salty tang tingles over my tongue. A stronger concentration of whatever lies on Cooper's skin. I need more.

My lips close over the head, my tongue runs along the join of cock and foreskin. So much tang, my eyes roll back in my head. All I can think of is smooth skin, solid strength, salty tang.

The baby-softness of the outer flesh hides the strength beneath. The taste of ocean is on his skin, with the slightest hint of neoprene. His thighs contract and release. I close my mouth over his cock and suck.

My mouth moves lower as I take him deep. An ecstatic high hums through me. My body feels light, filled with air, like a post-triathlon buzz. I'm slick between my thighs. I watch him watching his cock, and work on my rhythm.

The head touches the back of my throat and I breathe through it. Saliva runs, fills my mouth and slips down my lips and chin. My throat relaxes, anticipating the brush of his cock. I glance up and his eyes shut briefly before he meets my gaze. His eyes are almost inky black.

'Fuck. Keep going ... if you want ... but I'm going to lose it.' The gritty edge to his voice sends ripples of pleasure streaking through me.

I concentrate on suction, continuing the rhythm, taking him deep each time. Over the taste of my saliva and his flesh, a sweet salty flavour coats the back of my throat. My eyes wide, I glance at him but his head's thrown back, his Adam's apple bobbing.

Oh, God, he's going to lose it. I squeeze my thighs together as fluid gushes from my contracting cunt. If I slid a hand to my clit I'd come for sure, but I had my turn this arvo. This one's for Cooper.

I keep sucking and moving my mouth along the length of his cock. My tongue slides against the back, swirling over the rigid planes and throbbing veins. My hands on his balls stroke and fondle, before tugging gently.

'I'm going to come.' His voice is a strangled cry.

His cock slides down my throat in the usual motion and as the tip brushes the back of my throat, bursts of thick, hot, salty come fill my mouth. My lips close as I gasp. I pull back as I swallow, replacing my mouth with my hand. Sliding my hand on the slick length, I milk the last drops from his pulsing cock.

'Oh fuck. Fuck that's good.' His hand closes around mine, slowing the movement before he tugs my hand away and pulls me up along his body. My mouth is filled with the taste of his come. I don't want to finish. I want to lick every last drop.

'Holy shit, that was great.' His hand curves over my cheek and his lips meet mine. His tongue slips into my mouth and our kiss is hot and tender all at once. I wonder how he likes the taste of himself.

His hand slides against me, up and down along my back, soothing and arousing. His other palm nestles my cheek as he breaks the kiss.

'So good. I have to sleep.' His words come slowly as if he's struggling to stay awake. 'Sorry. Wait for...'

With barely a flicker of thick eyelashes against his cheekbones, sleep claims him. He looks delectable. Still strong and angular, but his muscles relax lending him a softer visage.

As much as I'd love to stay and catalogue his sleeping form, I need to leave. My sanity relies on me keeping the upper hand. That means leaving. I slip from under his arm, placing his hand on the pillow, hoping he'll think it's still my face. After dressing and grabbing my gear, I take one last look and fight to keep the sigh locked inside. I open the door and walk out into the cool night, carefully snicking the door behind me.

I don't imagine too many women leave Cooper.

Chapter 5

Thighs and calves burning, I push myself up hell hill again. I should have gone somewhere else but I half want to see Cooper and I hope he'll do the same run today.

I'm being ridiculous. I left him last night rather than staying and waking up with him this morning. Now I regret it. Yesterday was making a statement, showing my independence, being the different girl. Today I woke up horny, wanting to be fucked hard and sprawled across Cooper. I make no sense, even to myself.

Karma and this hill are a bitch. My lungs are burning, calves screaming and I'm not yet at the top. But damned if it's going to beat me. There'll be no slowing to a walk, no stopping for a perv, no rest in any form. I'm punishing my lustful body until it burns so hard from fatigue, sex is forgotten.

The summit looms and I spur myself on, hoping to get there before I expire.

I make it. Gasping, my lungs clawing for breath, I hit the top and slow down to an easy lope across the flat path. To the right a little way along is a viewing area and I hope to do some stretches and cool down there. And there's the entrance, tucked in behind some coastal shrubs.

It's not a fenced-off viewing area, only a cleared space with a magnificent view of the vast ocean with the diminutive dotted Admiralty Islands.

Lost in my thoughts and the scenery as I do my stretches, I don't hear Cooper until he's right behind me.

'Good morning, gorgeous.' His whole face is lit by his smile; his mouth framed with grooves, his cheeks raised and dimpled, his eyes shining brightly. I swallow to moisten my extraordinarily parched throat. He looks way better than the view—and it's spectacular.

'Good morning, I didn't hear you coming. Don't you ever puff?'

He laughs and his hand reaches towards my face while I'm caught in the middle of a calf stretch. Even if I wasn't stretching a leg, I don't think I'd have the willpower to avoid his touch.

'I had such plans for waking up this morning.' He's still grinning even with the slight rebuke. 'Only to find myself all alone, and my plans needed two.'

'You should never make plans. You never know what's coming around the corner.' I lift my eyebrows as I rise from the stretch.

'You've sure got that right. I've never been so wrong-footed as I am with you.'

I sink into another stretch. 'Is that bad?' I ask the question not knowing if I want the answer. But the answer doesn't really matter. This is a holiday fling. If he remembers me for being the one girl who kept him on his toes, that's not a bad thing.

He avoids answering by asking me my plans for the day.

'We're diving at nine thirty, lunch, then I have no plans. I thought maybe I'd snorkel some place.'

He nods and his grin deepens, making my insides mush. 'Too many corners huh?'

It takes me a long time to link his comment to my earlier one about not knowing what's around the corner. I blame it on his grin and my mushy innards. Too late to laugh, I smile vaguely. 'Did you have something in mind?'

He looks out to sea, following the flight path of a lone tern. I allow myself a few moments of perving. My gaze drifts across the squareness of his jaw, the power of the muscles in his solid neck, and the smoothness of that tiny dip behind his earlobe. His body fascinates me. Sheer bulk, complete strength, and utter delicateness all sitting side by side.

'I was thinking secluded. One of these beaches where no one goes. A picnic lunch we can eat after hiking. Then an afternoon spent snorkelling, sun baking, or whatever else might entertain you.' The grin is completely wicked and my body responds with a gush of sex juices.

Keeping him wrong-footed seems to be working in my favour.

'Sounds unplanned enough for me. Will I order lunch?'

'I hoped you'd agree. I've already taken care of it.' He has this look that's almost sheepish, as if he wasn't sure how I'd respond. Maybe my leaving last night unsettled him.

When I finish my last stretch I move against him and slide my tongue along his jaw. The rough prickle of morning stubble nicks my tastebuds. He still has the remnants of salty ocean and sweat. 'I do enjoy a man who can feed me.' I lick beneath his earlobe before nipping at the flesh.

'I enjoy a woman who can feed off me.'

My laughter rings out across the still morning air. 'Is that your plan for lunch?'

'You'll have to wait to find out.'

My mind fills with ideas and images. Eating from his abs, his arms, his chest, his back, his butt...

'Earth to Sam, you still here?'

My gaze snaps back to Cooper's and the heat of a blush races up my neck and over my face.

'Oh, I am going to enjoy lunch.' Cooper presses a light promise of a kiss on my lips and squeezes my shoulder. 'See you at the dive but I better finish my run or we'll miss it completely.'

He jogs off before I can assemble a reply.

The diving here is outstanding but a tiny part of me knows that more sex with Cooper may just outrank it.

***

After another superb dive, this time in Comet's Hole, we pick up our backpacks and head for lunch and seclusion.

'Have you found somewhere to go?' I ask as we head out of the dive shed.

'There's no guarantee of seclusion anywhere but they reckon North Beach or Middle Beach offer good possibilities.'

I stop. 'Middle Beach may be secluded but you can look down on it from the Valley of the Shadows.'

Cooper grins. 'I guess the choice is made.' We head north, hoping that others aren't so keen on the long hike when there are great beaches right near town. The trouble is that lots of active people visit Lord Howe in order to do the long walks.

'I'm in love with lion fish,' I announce before we've gone far. After spending far too long looking at them during the dive I feel the need to explain. 'There's something about all the frills and fins that fascinates me.'

'Don't worry. I'm fairly taken by them myself. They're striking with the black and white stripes and their elusiveness. I really don't mind you looking. I could spend all day playing with the coloured wrasse. I love how they get in your face and scout around. They're playful and inquisitive, and with that pointy, toothy mouth, it's like they want to talk, or grin, or nip you.'

'I've never dived with someone who likes the same things I do. Thanks. You've been the find of the trip.' There's no difficulty in giving him a saucy, playful grin. He's been the find of my life.

Cooper leans down close to my ear and whispers, 'You're just saying that because you think I'm good in bed.' With a quick swipe of his tongue, he moves away and I can do nothing but laugh. Loudly.

Probably not the reaction he was after but it doesn't stop him laughing with me. There's something exciting about a confident man.

The walk to North Beach is punctuated by dive and sport talk, short bursts of racing each other along the path, and lots of laughter. We stop to take a few photos because the beach is stunning, and even the photos are a time for mucking around. With Cooper I could be 12 again. At times we're like two kids fooling around in front of the camera, pulling faces, poking fun at each other. It should feel silly and immature but it doesn't. It's playful, easygoing, and feels more like foreplay than anything else.

When we get to North Beach, we hike up to the far end. Even though there's no one there, the rocks at the far end seem to beckon, whispering of seclusion, romance and mystery.

I spread out a couple of towels for our picnic lunch and Cooper pulls out tubs of food. As much as I'd like to eat my lunch from Cooper's abs, his words shut down any thought of that. 'I'm starving and I'm waiting for no one.' He dives for the food.

We eat chicken and salads with crusty bread. All fresh. All beautifully delicious. When we're done, I pack away the tubs.

'There's fruit somewhere,' Cooper says as I'm shuffling tubs into his pack. I pull out a container and can smell the mango with the lid still on. The sweet scent has my mouth watering, not only for the fruit. There are muscles on display here that could easily feed me mango. And he's lying down, shirtless. Perfect fruit platter.

I pick up a slippery slice of succulence. It's an effort not to drop it into my mouth but I stroke it down the mid-line of Cooper's stomach before following the juice with my tongue. A growl rumbles in my chest. My tongue tingles. I drop slices into the grooves between his abdominal muscles. Each breath Cooper takes has the buttery fruit wobbling, but none slip.

'Leave some for me,' are the only words Cooper mutters, softly and slowly before I lean down and feast from his abs.

Mango is sweet and soft with a texture of debauchery. Eating it from Cooper makes it so much more sinful, so much more delicious and so incredibly decadent. My lips touch firm skin, taste Cooper, then close over soft squelching fruit. My tongue licks over warm, tightly packed muscle that's sweet, salty and male. It confuses my head. Not just sensory overload but my senses are mixed. Soft and hard. Sweet and salty. Solid male and sexy squelch-like female. My head buzzes, my mouth zings.

I feed the last slices to Cooper. Easing the fruit between his lips and licking any escaping juice. When there are no mango pieces left, I lap each mound of abdominal muscle, each dip, until I can no longer taste the sweet dribbles of juice.

'I think you've peeled off layers of my skin with all that lapping.' Cooper's voice is a low purr. He's nowhere close to unhappy if his swollen cock is any indication. I've deliberately avoided touching it, leaving it to tent his boardies as I've feasted on other parts.

I lift my gaze to his, staring over his chest. 'I didn't hear too much complaining while I was eating.'

He flashes a grin and I wriggle along his body to capture his lips in mine. I straddle his stomach to get a deeper kiss and stickiness pulls at my inner thighs. I guess I didn't lap over the edges of his abdomen.

He sits up, kissing me throughout the impressive abdominal crunch, and settles me against his cock. The feel of it, hard, swollen and strong, tucked in against my heated core is heady. My hands slip behind his neck, fingers splay through his short dark hair, palms cradle his head, lips open, tongue dancing with his. I wriggle my hips in a slow stroke along his cock. His growl rumbles through his chest, along his tongue and into me.

He pulls back enough to turn the deep kiss into tiny nibbles. 'We need a swim,' he says against my lips.

It's a swim or getting naked as far as I'm concerned. And if he wants a swim, I can go with that. I wriggle from his lap and drag off my shirt and shorts. Holding hands, we run into the water yelling.

I don't know what it is about him that brings out my inner teen but she's here. Lusting after him. Laughing with him. Squealing and squirming. The best part is that he doesn't seem to mind. He's tickling, pushing, challenging and yelling right along with me.

The cool water splashes my heated flesh as we race in. And then we're diving, still holding hands. Water crashes over my head, my face, my shoulders, my back, legs, feet. We surface together, laughing. We brush water from our eyes at the same time which makes us laugh, pulls us closer together, makes me think how alike we are, how similar. How perfect.

And we merge. Mouth against mouth. Bodies entwine. Hands link, then drift apart, touching bodies, then fingers lace again. All the while the water drifts around us, pushing against us, but we're so entwined it can't slip between us. Cooper's chest is against mine, his stomach merged with mine, his legs twisted between mine. His hand slips up my back and in a flash, the clip for my bikini top presses against my spine before it's undone, followed by the strings at my nape. The soft fabric brushes against me in the swirl of water. His hand grabs it and shoves it into his pocket. Then he lifts my hips away from his body and untangles my legs. Water holds me, touches me, slips against me as he slides my bikini bottoms off and pushes it into his pocket along with the top.

Complete exposure to the water is sensual. Water caresses my thighs, slides along my nether lips, slips against my heated core giving wet kisses to my hot clit. Nipples, scrunched tight, are soothed by the gentle wet whisper against them.

Languid from the lapping water, I only half notice Cooper toss his shorts towards the shore. It's when his hands curve around my hips and he pulls me through the caressing sea to land against his naked strength, that I realise he's starkers. His cock juts forward to meet me before bending against my thigh and snuggling into the natural groove between them.

His hips cradle mine, his chest is the table for my breasts to fall upon. Our mouths meet, lock, explore. More moisture. The damp warmth of his lips is hot compared to the sea. The slow press of his tongue into my mouth reminiscent of the water's press into my cunt.

We're moving to the beat of the ocean, to the push and pull of the surf, to the ebb and flow. A slow sensuous dance.

When his cock presses against me, expecting entrance, I almost press down. I almost open to him in the hypnotic moment. Some part of my mind functions. I pull temptation away with a twitch of hips. The kiss goes on, the power of seduction stronger than my mind and again I'm wrapped around him, his cock begging for entry.

This time I twitch my whole body away, panting as I suck in air. 'Condom,' I manage to gasp. His eyes widen. 'Shit.' He runs both hands though his hair. He looks at me and shakes his head. 'Sorry.'

I move a step closer and brush my fingertips across his deliciously swollen lips. 'No need to apologise.'

He captures my hand and pulls it down into the water. For a moment I'm sure my hand will be pulled against him—his cock, his stomach—but his expression changes. His eyes gleam and his lips soften. A smile breaks across his face. 'Come skinny dip with me.'

A frown tugs at my forehead. 'Aren't we already?'

'We aren't swimming,' he says before he tugs me underwater with him.

Without having to speak, we race out further. Arms circling, legs pounding the water, heads rhythmically breaking the surface to breathe. His fingers brush mine mid-stroke and we both stop, treading water and breathing hard.

'I'm glad something makes you pant.'

He winks. 'It's someone, not something.'

Laughing, and thinking I have a good chance, I yell, 'Race you back to shore,' before plunging forward and swimming as fast as I possibly can.

When I'm almost to the shore I see the couple walking along the beach heading right to where I need to exit. Damn. Although I'm a body length ahead of Cooper, I'm not going to be able to claim victory by crowing on the shore. Treading water, I catch his arm as he comes up beside me.

'Seclusion's over.' I nod towards the people on the beach.

'My boardies are there.' He points to a lump moving in the shallows with each wave.

'Let's hope they aren't here to collect rubbish.' The grin on my face is quickly covered by Cooper's hot mouth. His lips hold mine while his tongue slips inside.

I pull away. 'Not here.' I shouldn't care; we've done more in public places before, but I saw the people. They won't leave my mind. I can't fall into Cooper's caress knowing I'm naked, there are people watching, and our swimmers are virtually at their feet.

We swim out to deeper water, away from people and the shore, where we can make out without disturbance. Long deep kisses, entwined with each other, the water swirling, is decadent. When we separate, the water encircles and holds me. I float with a sunshine blanket, a water bed, and my hand held by Cooper's. Bliss.

'Have you ever done underwater photography?' I give Cooper's hand a squeeze as I ask.

'No. You?'

'No. I've always wanted to. Are you interested in trying?'

Cooper's thumb strokes across my knuckles, another soothing movement in an ocean of them. 'Do you think we could hire gear?'

'We could ask tomorrow. I'm sure I saw a sign.'

'Will you get a camera too?' Cooper asks.

'Yes, I think so. Or should we work together?'

'Let's see who can take the best photo each dive.' Cooper's grin is almost a smirk, as if he's super confident that he'll be winning. He shouldn't be so sure.

'You're on.'

A kiss, and a lot of groping, seals the deal. Making out in the sea adds a fun dimension to sex but cools nothing. Together we're dynamite. It's a little disconcerting to find this in a holiday fling. He should be disposable, fun but non-threatening. Yet Cooper makes me think relationship, not fling. And if I think about that, I may drown.

When the kiss breaks I duck dive, needing the space underwater offers. Spreading the water with my hands, I push deeper, kicking hard. When my lungs start to hurt, I arch back and arrow to the surface, letting the water whoosh over my naked flesh. After Cooper's wrapped warmth, the cool openness of the ocean is freeing.

I break the surface and stroke away from shore, needing more space. Arms circling, legs pumping, I hit a rhythm that settles my mind. Running may stop my mind functioning, swimming gives me space to sort thoughts. I need a lot of sorting.

I swim until the pull of the ocean strengthens and lets me know I've left the shelter of the bay. I retrace my path back to shore. Back to Cooper.

Chapter 6

Early morning sunlight touches my cheek, warming me. The lightest brush of fingertips stroke across my stomach. My body wakes, alive, tingling and warmed by the great bulk of muscles wrapped around me.

Stretching, a smile on my face, I open my eyes and my lips. 'Good morning, Coop—'

His mouth devours mine, taking any words I would have said. After last night I'd have thought we'd have had enough of each other, but no. Last night seems to have only whet the appetite—both of ours, if this rampaging kiss is anything to go by.

It heats, quickly. In no time Cooper grabs a condom, sheaths himself and probes at my cunt. We're side by side facing each other. One of my hands on his abdomen, the other encircling his cock. I lift my leg and pause.

'We had sex like this last night.' I squeeze my hand on his cock, my other hand stroking downward towards his balls.

Cooper looks at me, his eyebrow quirked in question.

'Doesn't it get boring doing it the same way all the time?'

'Sam, nothing about you is boring. Are you bored?'

I need a brain transplant. I can't believe I began this conversation, let alone started it poised on the brink of more incredible sex. 'Never bored. You just spur me to greater things. I don't think we should repeat an act. We need to challenge each other to new things every time.' My hand cups his sac, weighing and lifting his balls, pulsing slowly against them.

Cooper's head shakes as his lips part in a grin. 'And you had to tell me this now?' When I make no sound, he adds, 'You're a very naughty girl.' His voice is full of cheek.

'I just woke up. My brain's not functioning.'

With a laugh, Cooper grabs both my wrists until I release him, then he flips me onto my stomach. 'Different enough for you?' He scoops my hips up and pulls me towards the edge of the bed. On my knees, head and hands against the bed, I turn to watch him, waiting to see what he'll do.

He slides out of bed and stands behind me, his eyes shining with excitement. 'Or do I need more inventiveness? Punishment, maybe?'

My heart jumps into my mouth. My backside is raised, at his mercy. And I've just said something ridiculous, which could deserve punishment. Would he? I lick my lips so I can open my dirt-dry mouth. 'Are you going to smack me?' Half scared, half excited, my voice quavers.

'Do you think you deserve it?' His tone is different. Sort of rough, a little harsh, thick with sexual promise.

I turn my head away from him and push my forehead into the mattress. How do I answer that? Yes, I deserve it for my timing. No, I don't want to be hit. But yes, I do want to.

The anticipation of his touch is making me giddy. Will it hurt? Will his hand cover all of my buttock? Will he use all of his strength? Will he slap or pinch or lick or swat or stroke? Oh, God, it's excruciating. 'Yes.'

'Yes what, Sam?' His voice is thicker, rougher, sexier. My juices flow. My butt's in the air, my legs apart, he's watching. He can probably see me getting wetter as he questions and waits. It turns me on even more. Shit. I can hardly breathe.

'Yes, I deserve to be smacked.' That is so not my voice. It's high pitched, breathy and almost a whisper. I'm no meek girl.

The air stirs, presses against my butt and then his palm connects. A sharp sting burns across my buttock, heat flares in the centre and spreads outwards. Before I can process the pain, the hurt, he's slapped the other cheek. Feelings flood. Sting. Pain. Burn. Tingling heat. Deepening desire. Flooding cunt. Clenched clit.

'Fuck, Cooper.' There's that meek breathy girl again.

His hand strokes from the tail of my spine upwards. 'Do you deserve more, Sammy?' His lips brush against the dip beneath my ear. His fingers curl through my hair, twisting it and lifting it from my neck. His tongue, wet and hot, slides across my nape. 'Would you like me to spank you again?'

Would I? I'm torn. I want ... what the hell do I want?

He rubs against me, his hard cock slides across my smarting skin.

'Yes, please.' It's that breathy girl again and I'm surprised that I agree with her. I want to feel the sting of his flesh on me. And then I want him to fuck me hard. The breathy girl vanishes when he bites my neck. 'After you punish me, you can reward yourself by plunging in and fucking me hard.' That sounds more like me, sure and cocky.

Cooper laughs a deep rumble in his chest. 'Can I just?'

He lifts from me, no longer connected. And this is what kills me. How do I know when he'll touch me? How do I know how much force he'll use? How do I know when to move to avoid it? Do I want to avoid it? Hell, this spanking has my brain confused. I want it, I don't. I trust him, I don't. I want it to hurt, I don't.

His palm cracks against my buttock loudly and flooding shame, joy, relief, horror, hurt and pleasure fills me. 'Argh!' It's everything I love and everything I hate.

His palm cracks against me again. 'Fuck!' Sharp, stinging, cracking. Setting my flesh on fire. The heat spreads, turns to pleasure. My cunt oozes, clenching in spasms.

His hands grasp my hips and with one hard thrust he fills me. We both emit a sound of part sigh, part burst of happiness. He holds still a few moments. Seconds where pleasure rockets through me.

He pulls back then impales me in one long deep thrust. I arch and push against him. Being filled is incredible but it's the marks on my buttocks that hold my attention. The stinging has moved to a deeper, dull throb that's filling my body. A beat I can't ignore. My hips roll and Cooper takes up the movement. His huge hands hold and direct as I move with him. His cock thrusts, his balls slapping lightly against my clit and pushing the air to move against it. Everything's screaming for release. Now.

My hand slips down my body so I can stroke my clit. The first touch has me jolt and Cooper nips against my shoulder blade.

'Yes, Sam. Make yourself come.'

Circling and flicking my clit, to my rhythm, while Cooper thrusts into me, is exhilarating. Every fibre of my being is caught in this push to orgasm. I rub gently and then harder, circling, stroking, flicking. Cooper's mouth on my back, lips kissing, tongue lapping, teeth nipping. His cock thrusting harder and faster.

With a squeeze of my clit between thumb and forefinger, I buck. Copper bites on the soft flesh between neck and shoulder and I scream. Pushing back against him, I convulse on orgasm. It fills my body. On and on. My finger keeps it going far past the usual release. My orgasm pulses; waves of pleasure, intense and dull, intense and dull, burst through me.

And then Cooper's cock pumps hard inside. And my orgasm flares. The intensity swamping me. Flooding me. I bite the bed sheets, clenching my jaw as wave after wave of heat fills me.

And then I'm sprawled across the bed. Feet hanging off. Collapsed in ruin. Gasping for breath, for sanity. Gasping to keep going, to keep riding the joy.

Cooper is over me, held up by arms bulging with muscles. Still filling me. Cock still twitching inside.

Neither of us says anything for the longest time. Neither of us moves. I'm incapable of thinking. I've been reduced to my basest self and I love it.

Eventually there's movement but I've no idea who moves first. Cooper strips off and disposes of the condom. I drag myself onto the bed fully, lying on my back with my head on the pillows. Cooper joins me. Without need for words, he holds me in his arms.

Our breathing matches. I close my hands over his. Secure in his arms, I snuggle against him.

Next thing I know, strong sunlight wakes me and a sound I can't identify. Cooper stirs beside me and then his eyes spring open. Dark chocolate pools. His lips break into a smile to rival the best sunrise. He kisses me lightly.

'I'll get rid of room service.' He slips from bed, drags on a robe and opens the door. A muffled conversation is background noise. My eyes are glued to the clock. Eleven, oh, eight. My mind can't make sense of the numbers. I lift myself up on an elbow and stare at the clock harder.

It's 11:08a.m. And I just woke up? Scratching my head, I still can't process. I never sleep late. Eight o'clock is a sleep-in. Has been for as far back as I can remember.

Cooper returns. 'Breakfast is here if you're hungry. As usual, I'm starving now I'm awake.'

I blink a couple of times before I can get words from my mouth. 'It's after eleven.' The words come out sounding like a question even though I meant it as a statement. Or maybe not. I am questioning it, along with my sanity.

'Lucky we have an afternoon dive today.' Cooper's grin is pure mischief. One that speaks of sated male, a night of great sex, and a morning of adventure.

I pull myself from the bed. 'I never sleep this late.'

Catching my hand in his, Cooper walks me towards him until I'm snug against his chest with his arms loosely around me. He kisses me lightly. 'Sweetheart. Until after six this morning, there was precious little sleep.' While his grin slides more towards gloating, heat slips from my chest up my neck and across my face. Why? I have no idea. I loved every minute of it. I have never spent such a decadent night, and maybe that's the reason for my tinge of shame.

'Come, eat. You'll need it.' Cooper holds a robe up for me, and after slipping it on, I follow him to the food.

***

I'm horny as hell in 15 metres of water, covered in a thick wetsuit, and watching a school of Moorish Idols dance around seaweed. Cooper holding my hand, my fingers interlaced with his, is not alone in causing my discomfort. Something changed between us this morning. Some dynamic shifted. I've always been aware of him, but now I'm hyper-aware. His gaze seems to lock onto and burn into me. His touch doesn't just brush against me, it leaves a tingling fire. His bulk doesn't just cast a shadow, it overshadows, has me wanting to meld against it, eager to taste, tease, and touch.

Something's changed within him too. He doesn't seem to care who sees us together. He holds my hand.

Slings his arm across my shoulder. Snuggles against my side. Kisses me in public.

I thought he'd hide our fling. I expected that with his public persona, he would try to keep me under wraps. Where earlier I had hoped that I might become a fond memory, now I'm hoping for more.

This change is making me think of other things.

That's a huge mistake.

I take my hand from his and tap the air gauge. If we want to see anything else, we'd better be moving along. I point my hand towards the edge of the rock wall and Cooper nods. We head back to the boat, checking out the rest of the rock wall along the way, but I'm distracted. Once I'd never have believed anything could interrupt my dive.

Cleaning the gear takes an age. Cooper brushes against me, touches me, laughs, whispers in my ear, murmurs along my neck. I could scream. I could run. I try to ignore him, ignore my arousal and go about normal business. It's difficult to concentrate, much less ignore him.

'We need to see about the cameras,' he says just as we're ready to leave. We were running too late to ask before the dive and I half expected him to forget. *I* had. I'm desperately seeking peace and sanity, away from him.

Arranging to hire cameras is easy. It's the lesson on how to use them that tries my patience, especially with Cooper's arm slung casually around me, his laugh shooting sparks down my spine, and his breath brushing across my skin.

Finally we're heading for home.

'I might head to my place for a bit.' I don't want to but I have to get control of myself and it's not happening when I'm anywhere near him.

'I don't think so.' Cooper's words are a low growl. Not threatening but determined. I stop and stare. 'I know what you need, Sam, and you won't find it at your place.'

My temper flares. My hands go straight to my hips and my jaw locks tight against the yelling I'd like to do. With cold precision I speak each word slowly. 'How do you know what I need?'

Cooper grins, eyebrows flicking, eyes dancing, lips pulled back so dimples slide into his cheeks. He takes my breath away. 'I've tormented you all day, Sam, teasing you until I can smell your need. But it's all in the spirit of doing something different each time. When we get home, you'll be right.'

'I'll be right?' I echo because his words make no sense to me. No sense at all.

'You're sitting on the edge, aren't you? It won't take much to tip you over? You smell like need. Hot, wet, strong need. I've just the plan for you. Come on.' He takes hold of my hand, tugging as if I'm a wayward child. 'I promise you'll enjoy it.'

I don't think. I don't question. I follow.

I can't work out what plan he could have where he'd need to spend all day teasing me. He can arouse me in seconds with a kiss.

There's no point in querying my reaction to Cooper. Initially lust drew me to his body but I know him now and it's not just his body I'm attracted to. He's the best damn thing to happen to me. The best vacation activity I've ever found. I'll never find anything like this again. He's the holiday of a lifetime.

It takes far too long to get to his place, get rid of gear, and have his naked body against mine, his mouth open to my probing, desperate tongue. When he steps back, I'm panting, trying to suck air quickly enough to devour him again.

'Steady. We have all night.'

'You might but some bastard has played me until I'm ready to crack. I can't wait any longer.' I do a pretty good impression of a growl, for all my breathlessness.

'You made the rules, Sam.' Cooper steps back and gives me the grin that turns my legs to liquid. I groan as I sink onto the floor.

I'm too old to have a tantrum but that's what I want to do. I'm like a two-year-old child frustrated beyond the point of comprehension. I want to thump my fists and kick my legs. I want to scream. But he's right. I did make the rules. I started this game of walking away after teasing ... Wish I'd known first that I was playing with a master.

'What's the plan, Cooper? You've got me at breaking point, now what?'

Cooper leans down and picks me up as if I weigh nothing. He deposits a kiss against my lips before I land on the bed. It's not arousing, not tender, not romantic, but Lord, it feels every one of those things.

'I want to watch you come.' He says it in the most matter-of-fact tone, yet they're possibly the most arousing words he could utter. As if I need any more arousal.

'What?' There's no demand in my question. It's more a request for clarification given in a whisper. I have no qualms about performing for Cooper. I openly admire his body and he, mine.

'I want to watch you. I want you to make yourself come and I want to watch you do it.'

My groan is low but full of lust. 'I could come just listening to you say that.' It would be so easy.

He shakes his head. 'I want to see you touch yourself, I want to know what you like, I want to watch you shatter and be there to pull you together afterwards.'

They are the most romantic words I've ever heard. Without further thought my hand slips between my thighs and I open my cunt lips with my finger and thumb, my forefinger stroking into the wetness as the lips part.

'Like this?' I ask as he growls, drowning out my words.

Expressive face and eyes, not only the growl, show me how much he enjoys this. His eyes—wide, dark and staring—ensure my exhibitionism gene kicks in. Spreading my legs wide, angled so he can see, my finger caresses, teases and torments not only me but him. When his lips part, his nostrils flare, and his mouth drops open, I press my fingers harder. Move them faster. Circle my vagina until I feel the muscles relaxing, the hole opening. Soaked with my juices, the scent heavy in the air, I keep stroking for him, for me.

Who would believe I could get off on this? I'm no prude. I've been sexually active for years. But Cooper's drawn out a different side of me and I adore this exploration.

His hand drifts over his swollen cock but doesn't stop, just a hesitation and then he leans on the bed with both hands, peering at me. His upper arms swell, forearms with sinews standing high. I slip my forefinger inside, making sure my legs are wide and angled for Cooper to see.

'Fuck, yes.'

'Why don't you join in?' I know he won't but I have a half-baked idea.

He shakes his head. 'I want to watch.'

'If you touch yourself, then I could watch you too.' My throat dries at the thought. Watching each other bring pleasure to ourselves. *Oh, please.*

There's a heartbeat of stillness where our gazes lock in a wordless tussle. While I wait for his decision, I slide my forefinger across my clit and the first wave of shivers pass through me. My eyes lose focus and then close, slowly, like the pleasure is too great to hurry. Cooper groans and the bed moves. My stomach clenches and I'm hoping his cock will fill me, but no smothering warmth comes close.

Opening my eyes I'm met by the sight of Cooper's cock clenched in his fist. His arm muscles bulge as he strokes steadily. And then he moves in a manner to make his pecs dance.

'Oh, God, yes.' My voice is worshipful and begging at once. Thick with lust. Dry with need.

He responds by sucking in a breath and his abdomen clenches. Cobblestones of muscles tensing and bulging across his stomach. I groan and his fist moves faster, his cock peeking out and then hiding from view.

I'm so slick, my fingers are soaked as I continue to alternately fill and frig myself. Waves of shivers turn to harder shudders as I watch Cooper's dancing muscles. I want more. So much more.

'Please, let me see your back.' Breathless girl has returned but Cooper doesn't seem to mind.

He turns slowly, his head twisting to keep me in sight over his shoulder. His back is awash with rippling muscles. His butt is two globes of high tensile muscle clenching and releasing rhythmically. My mouth hangs open, admiring the view.

'Don't stop, Sam.'

Oh, have I stopped? My fingers flex and move. Now one hand holds my lips open while the other is busy touching, probing, rubbing, filling. I wish I had another set of hands to bunch and squeeze my breasts and tweak and tug at my nipples.

As another wave of shudders runs through me, my head drops back, eyes closed, fighting the feeling, not wanting to lose control yet.

When I open my eyes Cooper's butt is clenched, dips hollowing on the outside above his thighs. Then his butt fills out to the glorious rounded domes I want to curl my hands around. My deepening growl has him repeating his butt dance. When I glance up, he's laughing at me, and I don't care. His back and butt are magnificent and I don't care that I'm panting while ogling.

'Are you close, Sam?' The butt dance stops and he turns towards me again, cock hard in his fist.

My hand, his muscles, his voice have me at the brink. All I can do is make an incoherent groan.

His hand fists his cock quickly, he takes a moment to spit on his palm and then fists faster. The muscles of his arms bulge, his chest flexes, his abs squeeze tight, and I'm there.

'Ahhhh...' Waves of pleasure burst through me. My finger rubs my clit to keep them coming. Wave after wave after wave. Pushing against me, lifting me, riding me high, high, higher. The roaring surf fills my ears, my mind is awash with sound and colours as I'm tumbled in the sea of pleasure.

And then I'm deposited on the sand, slid quietly to lie in the wash. My hands fall uselessly at my side.

A groan has me realising that I've company and I prise my eyes open to see Cooper's face a tense mask. His shoulders are huge, muscles bulging. Arms the same. And there's his fist, rigid. One held against his hip, the other still thrusting along his cock.

'Come on me, Cooper. Let me watch you come.' It's a reverent plea. One which has the desired effect.

The head of his cock beads and then a stream of white spurts. His fist loosens its grip and he milks the seed. A stream followed by dollops of hot come coat my stomach. I lift a finger and slide it through, coating my stomach in warmth. His eyes close momentarily and when they open, I lift my finger to my mouth and suck in the taste. Cooper's groan matches my own. There's something wildly decadent about tasting yourself and your man as one.

Chapter 7

I intended to leave sometime through the night. I don't want to fall into the habit of sleeping with Cooper completely. I mean, sex is fine, but staying multiple nights changes the fleeting nature of the game. It makes it more intimate and that's not something I can afford.

But somehow I'm still with him when the pre-dawn light wakes me. I'm snuggling against Cooper as if we're one person, spooning like we're never to part. His lower leg is thrown across mine, claiming me. His arm wraps around me, holding me close.

Damn.

I thought I could maintain perspective, keep this fun, make the sex competitive enough to leave him with more than just a vague memory of me in 10 years' time. But it's done something else. Along with being dive buddies, I've learned to trust him, to relax with him and to enjoy him. None of that is bad but it's only been five days. My body stiffens as I wonder if I've got myself into a situation I'll regret later. I have five more days and then I'll...

I squirm as lips nibble across my nape. A cock hardens, nestled against my butt. A hand closes over my breast and tweaks a tight nipple. A girl could get used to waking up like this.

'Good morning,' I murmur, and twist around to be caught up in a deep, compelling morning kiss. All concerns evacuate. My brain and body are filled with sex, desire, and pleasing my male god.

He has other plans. 'I'll be back,' he says as he pulls away and slips from bed. It's a soft promise carried across the early morning air.

I watch him walk away. That tight butt moves in rhythm with his back muscles, sinuously, sinfully. My mouth waters. He has an incredible body, a gorgeous personality, is a dive buddy you dream about, a bed buddy you never want to leave, and I want him like I've never wanted anyone before. *Hell. I'm in strife.*

Cooper's return stops my meltdown before it has time to really fire up. He places two bowls beside the bed, on my side. He leans over and grins that super sexy smile. My insides go all quivery and silly.

'You distracted me last night.' He punctuates with a wickedly delicious kiss. 'I had other plans but maybe they're better kept for now. Fruit and yoghurt make a delicious breakfast.'

'Yum.' Fresh fruit and yoghurt do make a delicious breakfast.

I go to roll over but he pushes against my shoulder. Then he lifts a spoonful of yoghurt and dollops it onto my closed mouth. Laughing, I lick through the dollop, poking my tongue out like a cat lapping.

While my mouth is half open, he tops the yoghurt with a strawberry poked through my lips. Moaning, I nip against the sweet berry, flavour flooding my mouth. I close my eyes for just a second as I savour and a splat lands on my stomach. Eyes wide, I find yoghurt on my torso, and Cooper's face grinning. He tops the dollop with a slice of pear standing tall in the yoghurt. A beautiful pear with deliciously feminine curves. While ogling the pear, a smear of yoghurt is spooned between my breasts. I squirm and the strawberry rolls from my mouth to land in this new yoghurt line.

'Nice touch,' Cooper says as he adds blueberries around the half-eaten strawberry.

He picks up a raspberry and with his face a picture of concentration, he aligns my nipple with the hole at the top of the raspberry. Gripping my breast, he fits my nipple to the raspberry and then does the same to the other side. My breasts throb from his touch and the tiny pressure of the berry cap.

My senses flood. The sweet smell of fruit is heady. The slightly sour, yeasty smell of yoghurt as it heats against my flesh reminds me of more carnal scents like me awash with arousal. I squirm, trying to squeeze my thighs together as if that would rid the room of my scent, but Cooper's hand slips around my right thigh and gently spreads my legs. His left hand drops a slice of mango onto my waxed mons and then he settles it between the lips of my wet, open pussy. He follows with a slice of paw paw. The soft, cool slickness and the musty smell overwhelms me. I moan, low and decadent.

The paw paw scent and the slick juiciness of mango are doing my head in. What other fruit could go down there? Nothing is more fitting. And then the laugh catches in my throat. Cooper has a banana in his fist. Catching my gaze, he slowly peels it. He is hot decadence, lusty mischief, and barely-reined-in anticipation.

My breath lodges when he slips the banana between my thighs. Insertion is my first thought and I'm squirming imagining that. How would a banana go inside me? How would he eat it out of me? My heart races and blood pounds, but it's mostly pounding around my clenched vagina. A throbbing pulse. Cooper's fingers press me wider. I hope he knows what this is doing to me.

One glance at his wicked, sexy grin and those dark, dark eyes and he knows.

He slides the banana longways along my slit so the tip pokes up above the mango and paw paw. Lord, it's like his cock pressing against me. My skin flares and the banana scent washes across. Cooper dollops yoghurt on my mons and tops it with a mix of berries.

'I think my breakfast is ready.' He licks his lips slowly. His stare captures and holds mine before slipping down my body. 'I'm not sure where to start. A meal has never looked so delicious.'

I think he should start on my lips, but then my nipples clench and maybe he should start there. The scent of banana drifts up and maybe that's where he should start. Oh, hell, he could start anywhere. 'Just start.' My voice is guttural, cracking on the last word, like a growl.

He chuckles and starts at my lips, probably to stop any further complaints. As if there would be any. Cooper's always starving and eats like a man who enjoys his food. There won't be another word of complaint from me.

His mouth is unrelenting as he kisses and laps the yoghurt from my face. It's almost a mutual eating as he licks and my tongue swipes. One hand cups his cheek and jaw, so I can guide his face nearer to mine, holding him so I can partake in the feast. My palm is scratched by the holiday stubble, rich and thick on his cheek. I can't help but rub my hand over his jaw. My fingertips explore the hardness of cheekbone, the strength of jawbone, the tension in the masseter muscles.

I groan when he pulls away from my face, yoghurt eaten. He turns his lips to my fingers and nips against them before his tongue sweeps across. Moaning again, my head is thrown back against the pillows while I fight the urge to squirm and wiggle. He drops my hand and I clench them into fists, holding still so the fruit doesn't fall.

His lips slide between my breasts. Hot, hungry lips on soft, tender flesh. He licks a big long stroke towards my chin and I gurgle with barely-restrained pleasure. He captures my hand with his, opening my fist and threading our fingers together.

Blueberries and yoghurt. The scent is subtle as he licks, laps and eats. My raspberry-covered nipples throb. Clenched tight they impatiently await his attention but he moves downward after cleaning the blueberries, nudging the half-eaten strawberry down my midline.

He eats the strawberry from my navel. I don't see but juice runs over the edge of my bellybutton and pools inside. He laps it, taking care to ensure every dip is followed by a swirl of his tongue that makes my back rise from the bed and my breath catch.

The pear is gone next time I look and he's licked away the yoghurt that held it. He moves further down and my thighs tense, my toes curl in anticipation.

Quickly, he bites the top off the banana and grins as if he's done something naughty and gotten away with it. In other circumstances I may have laughed but I'm too caught up anticipating the rest of the feast to manage it.

With a ravenous mouth he cleans the berries and yoghurt from my mons. He eats hungrily, his teeth rasping across my waxed flesh as he cleans up mouthfuls at a time, as if eager to get further. I'm a shuddering mess. My skin alternately tingles, throbs, and pulses. And when he's not touching it, it aches and burns for him. All the liquid heat of his mouth, his touch, makes me wriggle. Lapping the last bit clean takes no time. I almost wish there was another dollop of yoghurt. He stands and pauses.

Eyes dark with pleasure, he looks at the half-eaten banana and then at my raspberry-topped breasts. I dare not move. I don't want him to stop.

Finally, he prowls to the end of the bed and climbs between my thighs. Air whooshes from my mouth. He glances up from between my thighs and grins. God, he's pure sex when he looks like that.

His head burrows between my thighs and I'm lost.

I'm overwhelmed by scents and sounds. Banana awash with yoghurt, awash with me, awash with mango and paw paw. Traces of berries. The fresh morning air. The sounds of the sea whispering against the sand in the distance. The mashing of banana as Cooper feeds. The lap of his tongue as he scoops up yoghurt. The smack of his lips. The murmuring moans of a woman well-pleasured. A woman so far gone in ecstasy she's outside herself. The press of fingers into flesh. The slurp of mango juice. The suck of paw paw slipping through lips. The lap of juice and yoghurt. The scream of a woman's orgasm as male lips clamp her clit. The squelch of fingers slipping into a soaking cunt begging for filling. A rhythmic slurp of fingers fucking a wet cunt. And the low murmuring, swearing, panting, screaming of a woman's peak as she's pleasured beyond her wildest dreams.

Silence.

Stillness.

A suck as fingers slip out. The creak of the bed as a body moves. The soft growl as a man prowls. *Pop.* A raspberry is tugged free. The bright burst of raspberry juice. The tingling of a nipple until wet fingertips capture it. The slow suckle of a hot mouth on the other raspberry. The low murmur of a woman who can't possibly want more. The pop of a tight mouth pulled from a tighter nipple. A sigh, ragged and exhausted. The chuckle of a proud man.

I've experienced it all but I can't tell you any more. My mind is a wasteland of mush. Sensory overload has killed brain cells. My body is alive and screaming with pleasure but each body part is indistinguishable from another. I can feel my heart pounding, harder than after a race, yet I've barely moved. Muscles have wasted to jelly beneath my skin. I have no control over jelly.

I concentrate on the air moving into my lungs. My nostrils flare, cool air rushes in. I feel it slide down my throat and fill my lungs. I relax and the air parts my lips and escapes, warmer. I lie focussed on breathing until it again becomes natural.

'You're going to kill me, Cooper.' My words are tiny and quiet. Not like my voice at all. I could almost believe I'm defeated with a voice that soft.

'You set the challenge.'

I open my eyes to meet his amused gaze. 'I didn't know you were so competitive then.'

He grins. 'Bad luck.'

My mouth twists into a smart smile. 'Actually, I don't think it's anywhere close to bad.'

He laughs and wraps me in a hug, his lips meeting mine. The delicious remnants of breakfast are sweet on his mouth, before I recognise the taste of myself mixed in the blend. I stall as my flavour hits me. But his kiss demands my sole attention. He's devoured me as if I'm the sweetest fruit of all, and this kiss is no different.

***

I wish I could say I was sated but I can't. The more sex we have, the more I want. I hate to think how Cooper's feeling since he didn't get any direct relief but I'm not asking him or we'll never make the dive. Today the sea is like glass, so we're heading out to dive at the Admiralty Islands and I'm not going to miss it.

I'm glad of my determination. The dive is brilliant with calm seas, great visibility and loads of fish and corals to see and photograph. Back on deck afterwards, while assisting each other out of wetsuits, I chatter hoping to distract myself from lustful thoughts.

'Did you see that flutemouth at the end? Those tiny fins quivering a thousand miles an hour even though he was hardly moving. Wow. I've never seen one before. And my photo is awesome.'

'The long pipe fish thing?'

'Yeah, amazing wasn't he?'

Cooper murmurs an agreement but since I'm wrestling the wetsuit down his thighs I can't pay attention to his words, taken as I am by the play of muscles in his legs.

When he steps out of his wetsuit and starts on mine, all I can concentrate on is the puff of his breath across my nape and shoulders and the way shivers scurry through me. And then I realise he's talking to me.

'Sorry, what did you say?'

Cooper smirks. 'Are you off in Lustland again?'

I can't help it. I laugh even as a blush sneaks up my face. 'I'm trying not to go there but it sneaks up on me.'

'What was the bright blue fish with the yellow dash across the top?'

'A southern fusilier. Amazing colour, isn't it?'

'And those weird ones that were black with a yellow tail and a blue and yellow face?'

'Yellowtail angelfish. Related to the black ones with that blob of white halfway down their body that dart in and out of the weeds.'

'Oh, the skitty ones. They were funny. Racing around like they owned the place, then darting away to hide. I got awesome photos of all of them.'

I punch him in the arm before I remember how much it hurts. 'You won't beat my flutemouth.'

'What were the red-tailed tiny things that looked like they belonged in a tropical fish aquarium?'

'Firefish. I have a great pic of them too.' I strip my wetsuit from my feet and take it to the tub. When I return, Cooper is in deep discussion with one of the older chaps on the dive trip, receiving a lesson on firefish, scorpionfish, angelfish, scalybacks and Moorish Idols. I bite my lips to remove the grin and sit quietly beside him. Then I relent and hand him a water bottle hoping to break him away from his lecture but it's not to be. The man has a captive audience and Cooper is too polite to ignore him.

I stretch my back and lean my arms along the edge of the boat as we head back in. My fingers slide against Cooper's back, tracing the dips and troughs of muscle and vertebrae. I tip my face up towards the sunshine, close my eyes and let my fingers wander. Warm. Silken. Strong. Alive. Velvet-like. A hard nub. A slide. Flex, stretch, vanish.

A shadow falls across me and my lips tighten and lift before his heated mouth drops on top of them. It's a quick kiss. A brief brush. Claiming me before he sits back and soaks up the sunshine.

I hope I have some great photos of him too. Although you may not see much under all the gear, I love to watch his studied concentration as he lines up a shot, the intensity of his gaze while he examines. I love the outline of those hard muscles wrapped in neoprene.

And I hope like heck he doesn't think too much about the photos. I tried to make them arty or get a strange light angle. You don't take lots of photos of a holiday fling.

We unload, wash gear, do all the usual and then download the photos. There are bubbles in my stomach, a couple of wobbles in my knees, and a great big sense of satisfaction.

'You go first.' I wave Cooper towards the computer but he defers to my femaleness. Who am I to argue? I'm dying to see my photos.

Brian downloads them quickly and we begin the slideshow. The man who lectured Cooper about fish appears and stays to vote on the photos. We can't kick him out, although I'd like to. With my shoulders thrust back, a gleam in my eye and a heartbeat just a little too fast, I watch my photos flick up.

'Oh, that's good.' A nice Moorish Idol in a beam of light.

There's a few more of Cooper than I remember taking. My arms fold across my chest and I bite my lips. They are arty. And good, even if I have to say that myself. Cooper says nothing.

'Oooohhhh...' My flutemouth is stunning. In the dark background, with sunlight picking up his fins, it stands out even better than it did in the water.

Cooper lifts an eyebrow. 'You've set a high standard, Sam.' He's relaxed, head tilted back, eyes dancing, a lazy smile permanently attached.

A breathlessness takes over while I wait for his photos to download. The flutemouth is beyond my expectations. Surely he can't better it.

His early photos are all wrasse, scalybacks and angelfish. Hardly surprising as he loves these fish that dart around him. There are photos of me, not unlike those I took of him. No wonder he said nothing. My back muscles relax even as my heart gives a flutter.

None of his photos are better than my flutemouth. My back straightens, my chest puffs and a smile bursts across my face. And then his firefish appears.

'Shit.' The expletive pops from my mouth before I can think. His photo is incredible. Perfect composition, stunning lighting, and the firefish fills the shot as the dramatic hero. 'Coop, it's fantastic.' My hand closes over his forearm.

His expression is frozen. His mouth agape, eyes round and staring at the screen.

'Cooper.' I throw my arms around him and squeeze. 'You need to enter that into some contest. It's amazing.' I should be upset to lose again but the photo is incredible. Usually when you come back the magical quality of the underwater world is left behind, but with this photo he's brought it to the surface with him.

His body ripples before he turns into my arms. He hugs me. 'Sorry to whup your arse again.' His grin does what it always does and my insides go all gooey, my knees weaken.

I laugh, keeping it light because of the company. 'I don't like it but with you, I have to get used to it.' I've never enjoyed losing but competing means you have to learn to lose. I've had those lessons and now I'm being taught them again. It is a little easier this time, easier on the eye.

A big grin and a wink are my reward.

Brian and the fish man add their congratulations to Cooper. The fish man leaves while our photos are copied to a memory stick. We delete them from the cameras, ready for more competing tomorrow.

Walking out, Cooper links his fingers through mine and our palms meet. He holds hands like a hug; engulfing and warmth flows through.

'I didn't expect to beat your flutemouth, Sam. I can't believe I took that.' For all Cooper's fun gloating, there's this more serious side.

'I don't mind being beaten by a photo that stunning. You really do have to enter it somewhere.'

He nods. 'Maybe.'

I lean against him. 'Enter with a pseudonym if you're worried. It needs to be seen.'

We continue walking in silence for a while and then my competitiveness gets the better of me. 'Watch out tomorrow. I'll beat you yet.'

I sound happier and more confident than I feel. I'm wondering if I'll ever beat him at anything. Swimming. I can beat him at that. I'll have to race him in the water again.

'Oh, I'll be watching.' His look is unfathomable. Maybe he doesn't like to lose. Or maybe he likes watching me. I don't want to know. I'm not sure what sort of a loser he is. I suspect he'll be decent because he's a very respectable winner. It would be nice to win so I could see his losing form.

Walking home, hand in hand, in the quiet of the late afternoon, the sun is in my eyes. I don't have my sunnies and I should let go of Cooper's hand so I can shield my eyes but I prefer to squint. The thought sends darts into my chest. I swallow, deeply.

Cooper's voice distracts me from my latest panic. 'Do you think you could beat me?'

'At what?'

He shrugs. 'Anything, I guess.'

A laugh erupts. I hope he didn't mean that to sound arrogant. 'Of course I think I can beat you. I would have won yesterday if those people weren't there.'

He frowns. 'At North Beach?'

'Yes, I was lengths ahead of you. If they weren't there I would have beat you up the beach easy.'

'But they were. So we'll never know.'

'What would you give me if I did win?'

He considers my question. His gaze skims across my face. His step falters, slows then he stops, pulling me against him. 'If you beat me, Sam, I'd give you anything you want.'

'That's bloody confident.'

He smiles right into my eyes. 'I am.' Our stares remain locked for a long time. There's no answer I can think of but I refuse to back down. 'What would you want, Sam? What could I give you if you win? What's the greatest thing your heart desires?'

The intensity of both his gaze and his voice has my heart pounding. With his first question I was going to be flippant. The second made me stop to think. The third seeps into my soul, tendrils of hope weaving their way around my heart. I feel my mouth open. I know I am going to say something. I have no idea what it is.

'A child.'

The words spill. My heart clamps tight. My throat closes. My knees sag. I break from the stare, closing my eyes and screwing the lids tight.

Fuck no. Fuck no. Fuck. No.

I wrench my hand from his clasp. 'Cooper, I didn't mean that. I'd never.' His face is ashen. I could not have said anything worse. 'Shit. I'm sorry.'

I run. Paying no attention to where I'm going, bolting along the road, gasping breaths and cursing myself. I run out of road. I jump down the small drop to the beach and I run across the sand heading straight for the water. I drop my gear, shedding as I run and launch myself into the water without a care for my safety, without a thought. I stroke and kick. Hard. Stretching out, thrashing at the water, not caring about a rhythm, not caring about style or technique. I want to belt at the ocean until my life rewinds. I want to swim as far away as I can. I want to disappear.

I can't believe I said that.

I can't believe I want that.

I can't believe Cooper will come anywhere near me after this.

Chapter 8

When my breath comes in short supply, my arms ache with each stroke, and my legs are dragging rather than kicking, I turn and head for shore. My brain's sorted. My secrets spilled. My holiday fling shot.

Head low, I stagger up the beach to where I dropped my belongings, hoping they're still there. A shadow looms from the half-dark but I'm too exhausted to care.

Darkness? I hadn't noticed the light fade.

A towel wraps around me. I sink into an embrace so warm I snuggle deeper before my brain kicks into action.

'Jesus, Cooper. I'm sorry.' Before I can say any more, the pad of his thumb brushes across my lips then presses lightly.

'Don't say anything. Let me get you home and warm. Then you can talk.'

At another time, his words would be ominous. Tonight, I don't find them anything but a promise. I have apologies and explanations to give before I leave. It's a relief to have him willing to accept them.

After a shower, clothes and hot food, I'm snuggling into the lounge ready for sleep but I have to get the words out and walk to my place before I can close my eyes. I sit up straight, roll my shoulders and look at Cooper.

'I'm sorry for running, Coop.' When he opens his mouth to speak, I hold up my hand. He stops and I continue. 'And for swimming for hours. I scared myself. I had to process and I do that best swimming. I apologise that I didn't think about you. I didn't expect you to wait. I'm sorry I put you to that trouble.' I drop my hand into my lap. 'Thank you for looking after me. It's more than I deserve.' I lean over to kiss his cheek and then I stand.

'Why does this sound like goodbye?'

I pause as I bend down to gather my gear. 'Um, because it is. I'll see out the rest of the dives but I think it's best to leave it at dive buddies now.'

He's off the couch and has my wrist snagged in his hand. I jerk up but don't pull my arm away, his grip isn't tight. 'What if I have a different opinion?'

I pull my lips together and tuck them into my mouth. My brow furrows and I feel the need to squirm under the intensity of his gaze. 'I'm willing to listen.'

He gives a tight nod, but I need to explain. 'I scared the hell out of myself back there, Coop. I didn't for a second think about what I was saying. I'd never trap you into having a kid. I know you live for football. You were upfront about that. I ... um ... I didn't realise I wanted that ... um ... quite so much. I wish I could forget I said it.'

Cooper leads me back to the lounge and sits beside me, still holding my wrist. 'I think you scared yourself more than you scared me.'

I spin to look at him, mouth and eyes wide.

'In the past week, you've never taken advantage of me. You've been an awesome dive buddy, a great bed-and-other-places buddy.' He gives me that one-dimple sexy grin before continuing. 'I thought our conversation was light-hearted and fun until you bolted.' I drop my head, staring at my knees, mentally cursing that I'd run instead of laughing. 'Sam, footy's still my life but I'm 30. I know it can't always be.'

In all those words, I should have another question but what spurts from me is, 'You're 30?'

Cooper chuckles. 'What did you think I was, 15?'

I laugh and tension releases. Muscles relax across my shoulders that I hadn't noticed were clenched. My neck muscles loosen. 'I was pretty sure you were legal.'

He swoops in and kisses the tip of my nose. 'That's a relief,' he says with a big melty grin. The pad of his fingers brush beneath my eyes. 'You're stuffed, Sam. Come to bed and talk about this tomorrow.'

'You still want me here?'

'You aren't that scary, Sammy.' He tugs my wrist before picking me up and carting me across to the bed. Instead of tossing me on, like he usually does, he lays me softly and places the gentlest of kisses to my lips. 'Sleep. I'll be with you in a sec.'

I wish I waited for him but the next thing I know, it's sunrise. My time of the morning, when the sun peeks above the horizon and the sky wakes. I stretch, trying not to wake Cooper who sprawls beside me.

He's beautiful. On his back, one arm thrown above his head, the other out to the side. His legs are apart, a sheet straggling across his hips and over part of his legs but his feet poke free. The rise and fall of his chest is mesmerising. A peaceful rhythm moving his torso as if it's washed by waves. Dark brown nipples punctuate his pecs and call silently to my lips. I don't want to wake him but I can't resist their cry.

I twist my hair into a knot to stop it brushing against him. Leaning over, careful not to touch him except with my mouth, I close my lips over the nearest nipple, his right. My tongue laps across the top, before tracing around the cylindrical nub. It stiffens, allowing me to suckle.

A slow hiss of air and I realise Cooper's awake, or at least waking. My hand slides from the bed over his hip and onto his stomach. My fingertips reach beneath the sheet.

142

'I'm glad you stayed, Sam. I could get used to waking like this.' The husky morning voice prowls down my spine. It's warm, rich, deep and tinged with sleepiness.

Sucking on that nipple, flicking with the tip of my tongue, I sneak my hand under the sheet before curling it around his cock. Then a slow squeeze as I bite his nipple. His groan sends shafts of need through me. There's major muscle tension across his chest and abdomen. I bite and nip my way from his nipple to his groin, all the while squeezing and releasing his hardening cock.

I remember what happened yesterday but I shove it aside. I want him. I want to give him this. I want more than the memory of me being an idiot, and so must he. I want to be remembered for great sex, not a stupid meltdown from a thoughtless comment.

While licking around the base of his cock, small moans fuel my interest in making him wait for my full mouth. I wriggle to slide between his legs, ensuring access to all areas. My other hand runs along his thigh, stroking the soft skin at the top of his leg, then the wrinkled sac of his balls. I pinch the excess skin between thumb and forefinger as I lick up the side of his cock. There's only a catch in his breathing. I have to try harder.

Next time I slide my tongue along his cock, I cup his balls in my palm, weighing, lightly kneading and tugging. I get the groan I was waiting for and reward him by holding my lips around the top of his cock, breathing out slowly to push warm air down his shaft.

'Sammmm...' Begging with a breathy moan.

I only flick my tongue across the head.

'Please.'

I love hearing him beg, it makes me want to bring him to his knees. After yesterday, I owe him glorious, fantastic morning sex.

Taking his cock fully into my mouth, I add suction as I press downward. I feast. Licking like I'm scooping dripping ice cream. Sucking as if I have the longest straw. Taking my time. Mixing up mouth movements. Allowing saliva to flood his cock while my hand curls tightly around the base.

My other hand plays with his balls, strokes his thighs, pushes his legs wider for better access. My fingers stroke, pinch, nip, tease and explore. I'm listening for breath catches, moans, a groan, a sigh, a word. Paying attention for signs of pleasure: muscles tensing, breath speeding or stopping, legs wriggling or squirming, arms tensing, hands clenching. Cooper's responsive. It's easy to know what he likes. Sometimes I give him more of what he likes, other times I give him less. It's no good making it predictable, much more fun making sure he doesn't know what's happening next.

When he's lost in my blow job, I take my fingers on a tour of the darker areas of his body. I've always been interested in anal exploration but it's not something you can do with a one-night stand, and certainly not with everyone.

Cooper's open, expressive, fun, and easygoing. He gives me the confidence to slide my saliva-slickened fingers across his perineum and around the sphincter of his anus. A deep gravelly moan, along with the quick tensing of muscles as he lifts his hips towards my mouth and fingers, encourages me further. I press my wet finger to his butthole.

A muffled cry, not a groan of pain but not one of pleasure either, spurs me on. Sucking hard, his cock deep, touching the back of my throat as it bobs, I keep the pressure on the sphincter. My finger eases in as the muscle relaxes.

'Oh God.' His voice is strangled, caught somewhere inside him. But he's not asking me to stop. He's not in pain. It's like he's writhing along the pleasure-pain continuum and I know that can be a mind-blowing ride.

Lifting my head, I drag my lips and tongue up the length of his shaft as my finger pushes a little deeper. I haven't yet reached the first knuckle but I can feel the ever-tightening grip of the anal sphincter. He's not completely relaxing into this yet.

Saliva runs down the length of his cock as I hold the head between my lips, my tongue slurping around the dome. I open my fingers clasped around the base so warm saliva can trickle over the perineum. More moaning fills the air as my tongue flicks at the slit on the top of his cock. Probing lightly with tongue and finger, a deep sense of satisfaction rolls through when he bucks into my mouth. His anal muscles relax enough to let my finger slip past that first joint.

'Fuck. Take me deep again, please.'

I hesitate for long seconds. Nothing moves. My finger is still, teasing his tight arse. My tongue is tucked away, not touching his cock. My lips are sealed around the head, holding nowhere near firmly enough. My hand is loose around the base. I'm tormenting him, he knows it, and I can only hope he loves it, or at least thinks that suffering through it will be worthwhile. A sly smile twists my lips when I meet his tortured gaze. His eyes are almost inky, eyelids narrowed, tension marring his forehead and the edges of his face. He doesn't look like he wants to wait any longer.

The power is indescribable. I literally hold this man's pleasure in my grasp. He trusts me. He's handed his body to me. Nothing is a better aphrodisiac. I'm on an orgasmic high without him having laid a hand on me.

'Please, Sam.' The words are forced from his mouth, past teeth clenched tight.

I tighten my hand around the base of his cock and slip my finger out from his arse. While sliding that finger in the pooled saliva, I open my lips. His eyes widen. I slowly sink over his cock. His eyelids droop as my lips lower. By the time his cock is buried in my mouth and my lips are tight around the base, his eyes are clenched as tight as his jaw. I suck while my head bobs up and down. I slide my tight mouth right up his cock, then while paused at the top, my finger presses against his sphincter. In a simultaneous act, my mouth slides down and my finger pushes inside and upwards to put pressure on his prostate gland. Sucking while the head of his cock strokes the back of my throat, the salty semen taste almost makes me gag. I ease off and pull my head back. Then I try again without the gagging. All the time rubbing over the prostate or lightly tapping against it.

'Fu ... nooooowwwww,' is the only warning I have before his cock spasms and come jettisons against the back of my throat. I suck it down, my hand milking his cock while my finger presses. His hips rock into my face, fast and hard but I control his cock. He can't thrust it down my throat as my hand protects the depth. I'm free to milk him dry and suck every drop. And when I do, I slip my finger out and ease my hold on his cock, lifting my head and lapping the last drops.

There's just the deep rasping pant of Cooper's breath to break the silence. I go to the bathroom to wash up while he recovers.

I don't think I could have redeemed myself better. A debt has been repaid, though I know it's crazy to feel indebted and Cooper would no doubt argue with me if he knew.

I walk back with a warm facecloth to wipe him. His eyes are still closed but his breathing is back to normal. As I pad beside the bed, he opens first one eye, then the other, almost squinting at me.

'I think you killed me, Sammy.'

I smile and drop a kiss on his lips. 'I have a warm cloth. It might make you feel better.'

'Sweetheart, nothing will make me feel any better than I do right now.' A lazy smile pulls against his lips and the dimples give me a kick in the stomach. *God, he'd make cute babies.*

To distract my thoughts, I quickly wipe him with the cloth, first his cock, then between his legs and his butt. When I finish he grabs my wrist and tugs me down beside him. He takes the wash cloth and tosses it through the bathroom door onto the floor.

'Thank you.' His stare captures me and penetrates right into my chest. When I blink, his mouth closes on mine and his kiss sends ripples of pleasure through me. His kiss worships me. It wraps me in him, twists me around him, and curls my toes. His tongue mates with mine. The kiss is a never-ending swirl. An eddy dragging me into the frenzied centre. And I'm floating, although I should be drowning.

We break the kiss but remain lying sprawled across each other, catching our breath. Cooper's hand strokes along my spine, mine cradles the back of his head and his shoulder.

'You didn't have to do that.' His gaze challenges me, as if daring me to argue.

'I wanted to.'

'Because you felt guilty?'

I bite my lips together and shake my head. 'No. It's part of the challenge. A different form of sex.'

A frown mars his forehead. 'Oh.' The frown deepens and the muscle at the back of his jaw tenses for a long time before releasing. 'Why did you do that?'

My head drops to the side, trying to work out what he means.

'Why did you ... finger me?' The hesitation and the low volume tell me there's some discomfort. But I am one hundred per cent certain he enjoyed it. So the discomfort must be psychological, not physical.

A smile dances across my lips and I try to rein it in, unsuccessfully. 'It's not that I think you're gay. Geez, nothing would make me think that after the last few days.' He doesn't yet have a grin matching mine, so I'd better keep explaining. 'I've always wanted to explore the darker side of sex and you seem receptive to trying things. I thought you might enjoy it, and if not, I figured you'd let me know.'

'So...' He pauses, as if not sure how to proceed.

I jump in. 'Coop, seriously, it's no big deal. It's between us. Our secret. It's been done once, so I'll never do it to you again.' I press a kiss to the stress lines at the corner of his eye. 'Besides, I thought you enjoyed it.' I grin, or maybe it's more a leer.

He shakes his head, not in a negating way, but as if shaking bad thoughts from his head. 'Sorry. I'm just being an idiot. I did enjoy it.'

His reaction is all wrong. He should be soaking in a post-orgasmic high, yet he's on a down and I've got the high. It must be still about yesterday.

I draw a deep breath. 'I do feel guilty about yesterday. Not only what I said but my bad reaction too. I'm sorry.'

His arms come around and wrap me against him, nose to nose, toes to toes, and everything between lining up.

'Yesterday is fine, Sam. I get you want a kid but haven't admitted it before. I know you won't take advantage of me because you haven't already. It's cool.'

Relief surges through me, like gusts of fresh, clean air after a storm. I murmur my thanks and wriggle closer, brushing my nose against his, my lips over his. 'If it's not that, what's wrong?'

'I'll trade you secrets.' He pauses, takes a deep gulp which has his neck shifting and his chest heaving. 'There are always rumours about my sexuality. I thought maybe you were testing them.'

You could have knocked me over with a feather. I'm sure my face shows my surprise. 'Testing rumours? Why would people need to comment on your sexuality?'

He shrugs before answering. 'I don't splash my sex life around for the world to see. I don't have women hanging off my arm at every event. How would I know how they think?'

Before I can scoff at his fears, the image of him coming to wrap me in a towel fills my brain. Last night my fears were irrational and badly dealt with. I can't criticise him for this. 'Coop, I didn't even know who you were. And I'm embarrassed to say I still don't know anything about your fame. I wouldn't know what rumours there are. I like sex. I like to know what turns people on. I'd read about perineum stimulation and prostate massage and I've always wanted to try it. I didn't think you'd mind.'

He rests his forehead against mine and gives me a squeeze. 'I didn't mind at all, until my stupid brain kicked in.'

'Would you like me to keep all the attention downstairs so your upstairs brain doesn't have to think?'

Finally, Cooper laughs. A proper laugh. One that tells me he's over the panic my actions caused. He swoops a kiss on my lips, then nuzzles against my jaw, beneath my ear, down the side of my neck. Everything begins to feel right with the world.

I can't imagine what he went through yesterday while I churned the lagoon. His freak-out lasted bare minutes and had my heart thundering. He's made of tougher stuff than I.

Two freak-outs. Two secrets exposed. And we got through them.

So much for the simple holiday fling. This is getting more like a relationship. Something I wasn't prepared for. Something Cooper doesn't want.

Chapter 9

After all the craziness, a morning run across the flatter parts of the island before the dive seems too normal, but normality is good. The run settles me. We're back to light-hearted teasing by the time we pick up the cameras and gear. No one would guess the intensity—or the insanity—we've shared since the last dive.

Today's dive is at the magnificent Balls Pyramid. A rock, over five hundred metres high, sticking straight up in the middle of the ocean. It's as beautiful above water as below. Another site filled with fish and ample opportunities to snap the winning photo. I don't. Cooper has the best shot again. It's not that my photos are dreadful, it's just that his are spectacular.

'You take these shots without mucking around. How?'

Cooper grins, waggles his eyebrows, and mimes zipping his lips.

'Oh, come on,' I plead.

'Natural talent.' He shrugs. 'I honestly don't know, Sam. Something catches my eye, I line up and snap.'

'So, if you didn't play footy, would you be a photographer?'

Cooper laughs loudly. 'Now, they're two jobs that no one else would put together.'

Over a late lunch we continue discussing photos. I keep trying to work out how I can beat his brilliance. I'm not sure I can, but there's no way I'll give up.

After lunch, we snorkel in the lagoon below the two huge mountains at the southern end of the island. And then we head back to Cooper's place.

'Have you climbed Mount Gower?'

I shake my head. 'I've thought about it but haven't stopped diving long enough to do it.'

'You can't dive on your last day. Should we do it then?'

'Yeah, if we can. We have to have a guide and go in a group. I think they only go one or two days a week.'

'No problem. I'll find out.'

'It's a full day. Will you mind missing a dive?'

'Sam, I don't know that I'll bother diving when you go home. I'll only be here a couple more days.'

'What will you do instead?' I'm worried that I've had him diving more than he otherwise would have.

'Probably sit and sulk because you've left me.'

I spin around and stare. Words fail me.

Then he chuckles. 'I'll snorkel, run, take photos, roam around.' He shrugs. 'I'll do whatever I would have done had you not...' His hesitation makes me laugh.

'What? Crashed your holiday? Distracted you from resting? Made you do a thousand dives you'd never have otherwise done?'

'No. Well, yes. But all in a good way.' We're back at his place and stop at his door. He studies me for a long time before he says, 'I've done much more diving with you than I would have but I've loved every minute. Usually I only tolerate my buddy which doesn't make it as much fun.'

'Phew.' I flash a grin. 'For a minute there I thought I was dragging you to do something you didn't want to.'

'As if.' He drops a kiss on my nose. As he steps closer to deepen the kiss, I interrupt.

'What's for dinner?'

'No plans. You?'

'No plans.'

'Will we go back to your chowder place? You must have withdrawal since we haven't been back there.'

I chuckle. 'No withdrawal, but it does sound good. I'll head up to my place and get changed. Will I meet you up there?'

'What's the rush?' He's already standing close enough to be a coat. Within a blink, his lips are against mine, opening them. His tongue touching, teasing. His body moulding mine. Our kisses are an explosion in waiting. No longer enough in themselves, they're a precursor. Full of anticipation and promise.

The door flies open and we stagger inside without breaking the kiss. Cooper must have opened it while we were kissing. Clothes are shed before we make it to the bed. The door bangs shut. Naked, touching, rubbing and writhing, the kiss moves towards imitating sex. Deep penetration, thrusting, sucking and nipping. I cannot get enough of him. As close as I am, I need to be closer. I need him a part of me.

I grab a condom as we pass the bedside table. My leg shinnies up his before clasping around his hip. I'm angling my hips so I can push myself onto his cock when he stops and pulls away.

'We've done it like this.'

Fuck. I can't believe he's throwing my own stupid words back at me. Now. 'I don't give a rat's, Coop.' I manage to grate the words between clenched teeth and knotted jaw.

His deep, throaty chuckle spears from my ears to my pulsing clit, not helping my need one skerrick. Open-mouthed kisses move from my lips to my jaw, ear, then along my neck and across my shoulders. He steps around behind me, his cock, hard, sliding against my buttocks. I groan before the length settles into the natural dip between my cheeks. The open-mouthed kisses work back towards my ear.

'I've been thinking about this all day,' he murmurs. I moan my agreement. 'You said you wanted to explore the darker side ... does that include me giving it to you?'

An internal giant fist grabs hold of my stomach region and squeezes. I can't breathe. I can't swallow. I can't think. I have to make some sound. I have to see what he means. If he means ... *oh God.* A long guttural sound that should belong in a dark forest on a stormy night escapes me.

'So I could give you anal and you wouldn't mind?' he asks quietly.

The condom drops from my fingers.

That internal fist twists until the breath hisses from me. 'Yes.' His cock leaps against me as he growls against my ear. His teeth nip my earlobe and his hands splay across my buttocks. Liquid heat gushes down my thighs as my clit and vagina pulse.

His hands slow and his lips move away. I have a few seconds to think. 'Have you done this before?' I ask, turning to look at him. When I catch the downward flick of his gaze, I quickly reassure. 'It doesn't matter if you haven't. I just want to remind you of one thing.' I hold up my forefinger. 'This is what went into your arse.' I hold my finger about half way. 'This far.' I look down at his cock. When I stare back at him, he's a paler shade. That wasn't my plan.

'I'm not scaring you off, Coop.' I turn and catch his jaw in my palms, holding his face so he remains looking at me. 'I want your cock buried inside me.' His eyes darken, pupils expanding. 'I just want you to take it slow. Let me adjust to the size. No ploughing in. If I scream, you stop.' I don't honestly think I'll have to scream but it's worth having it out there. Cooper takes his time, pays attention to my reactions and knows how to handle his cock. I have no true fear but I've given the reminder.

'I'll look after you, Sam, I promise.' He doesn't need to promise. The raw honesty is there in the intensity of his gaze, the soft curve of his mouth, the tightening of his jaw.

Our lips lock, meshing together in a frenzy of desire. He walks me backwards until my legs hit the side of the bed. The kiss doesn't stop. We stand beside the bed, devouring each other. My body's dying for more but savouring each moment. It's a delicious place to be, caught between enjoying what you have now and eagerly anticipating what comes next. It makes my skin dance and my heart cha-cha.

We break for air and Cooper grabs condoms and lube from the side table, throwing them on the bed. I pile up pillows. With my back to him, his hands catch my hips and slide upwards, fingers brushing against the underside of my breasts before sliding higher and catching my nipples. He rolls them between his fingers and a moan shudders from me. His cock presses between my buttocks, not just against them. When I bend over the pillows without resting on them, Cooper's hands still on me, his cock aligns with my open cleft. And it feels so damn good. Long, thick, hard and warm. I want more than just the pressure of it against me. I want to feel it probe, push, enter. But I want to bask in the now. The exquisite touch on my nipples, the heat from his body, the slow burn of need welling inside.

I slip my hand backwards and curl it around his cock, angling my hips so I have the space to manoeuvre it. I guide his cock along my cleft. From the top down, across the sensitive anus, over my soaking vagina but not so far as my clit. *Damn it.* I need to be bent more so it can reach my clit. A growl vibrates in my chest as I slide the head of his cock across the slick heat of my cunt.

'If you want slow, you better stop doing that.' His growl makes me chuckle. Teasing him is one of my great pleasures, but not if it'll end up hurting me. I drop my hold on his cock.

'Have we got time for this before dinner?' The words fill the room and it takes me a couple of seconds to realise I've again made a completely inappropriate, badly timed comment.

'I don't give a fig about dinner.'

I gasp before snorting a burst of laughter. Cooper swats my right buttock, bringing my mind back to sex. Stinging, smarting sex.

'What happened to the man who had to eat all the time?' He upends me on the bed and scrapes his teeth across my stinging butt cheek. The sharpness of teeth on the reddened skin shoots unexpected pleasure into me. 'Oh God, yes.'

'I got hungry for you.' He picks me up by my hips and settles me firmly onto the pile of pillows. 'Like this?'

I'm unsure if he's asking me to get comfortable or waiting to feast further. I wriggle until comfortable, head and shoulders down, butt high, legs apart ready for him. And I murmur 'Yes,' just in case he needs my approval.

The bed bounces as he leans on the end. I'm positioned so he can remain standing and my butt should be the perfect height. At least I hope so. But he'd say if it wasn't right, even if he's a little more shy than I am.

The air thickens while I wait. I can feel his breath against my skin but that's the only connection. A warm drift of air across my right buttock. A quick burst of breath against my right inner thigh, as if he's sighed. A directed jet across my dripping cunt as he blows over it. And then a puff of air against my anus which has my body clenching.

Oh, I want him. I want to feel him pushing hard into me. So large, so solid, so...

Thought suspends as my body rocks with the movement of the mattress under his shifting weight.

His tongue slides across my arse.

God. Warm wet wicked wonderfulness.

Again.

A purr rumbles from deep inside me and spills across the pillows and sheets.

Again. A slow, long, wet lick. Straight across. Like he's a cat checking out his food before eating.

Again. This time slower. A little harder. A lot wetter, although that could be my imagination compiling all the wetnesses together.

Again. This time it causes my body to bubble. A cry bursts out as his tongue probes my tight hole. Wet. Hot. Pressure.

A rest while I pant. 'Not. This. Slow. Coop.' My words get caught up in my breaths.

His mouth comes down on me again, a wet slick of his tongue, then his teeth press into the side of my buttock. Red flares in my brain. Hot need pulses. My cunt contracts and holds tight. My breath is captured.

A burning sting with a sharp crack. My left buttock comes alive. His teeth move on my right, biting in a different place. Both cheeks burn, sting and throb.

Then his hand slips between my thighs and a moan escapes before his fingers plunge into my sodden heat. His fingers stroke along my lips, holding them open while one dips into my vagina, then two. He scissors them inside me, while he slaps me again. I fight my orgasm. I fight it even as it threatens to consume. I stare unblinking at the bed head, focussing on anything but the pleasure. His teeth let go of my butt. Thank goodness. I breathe. I want to draw this out. I don't want to come so quickly. I want...

He slaps again, while his fingers thrust inside my cunt and his tongue probes fast and hard into my anus. No warning. No preparation. No time to stop the tidal wave.

Pounding emotion consumes me. All my holes compress. My clitoris tattoos its release. A throbbing beat that drags me upwards, higher than I expected, and holds me suspended while his tongue licks across my hole, back and forth, nerve endings fizzing.

'Cooper.' His name comes out in a thousand syllables before I fall back to earth.

Kisses brush across my buttocks, along my thighs. His hands hold, caress, pinch and touch. All the time I'm catching my breath, and wanting more.

Before my breathing is normal, but after the panting has ceased, a cold wet chill hits my heated flesh. Cooper's hands spread my buttocks, his left holding me open, while his right dips and massages lube into me. Another groan fills the air. Me. Again.

I grab each cheek and hold them apart, so Cooper can focus all his attention on touching me. I've become desperately needy.

His fingers have me writhing. Strong and thick, they push and probe. I'm spread for him and he ensures every part is explored. From my pubic bone to the end of my spine. I'm burning. The lube is no longer cold as it heats from the sizzle of my skin. God, never have I been this far gone before. I'm incoherent.

And then his finger pushes against my anus. I tense, for a long moment. Breath held, unsure. A finger taps at my clit before circling, tapping, circling again. My focus switches. Tension bursts and I'm left arching, then pushing back on his finger. The middle knuckle pushes in and I cry out, half pleasure, half pain. My butt clenches, then releases. His finger works its way out, then slides gently in. This time it's all pleasure as my muscles relax to his touch.

'Oh, please.' Begging does not become me but right at this moment, I don't care one whit.

'What do you want, Sam?' So much emotion in that voice and if even half a brain cell was working I could identify those emotions. Need. Lust. Pleasure. Those come to mind but maybe that's because they're what I'm feeling.

'Tell me what you want,' he says as if that's a simple request.

How the hell can I answer that? I want more. I want less. I want him fucking me. I'm happy with his fingers. I want to be stretched more. I'm happily stretched now. 'Fuck. I. Don't. Know.' Each word is pushed out as I gasp for air and sanity.

His response is neither a chuckle nor a cough but somewhere in between. More lube. The cold shocks me for a second before it heats. More pressure on my anus. I pant through the push and arch again as the pain gives way to flooding pleasure.

'You'll tell me before it hurts, won't you?' If Cooper thinks I won't, he's crazy. I nod. Words are too much effort. Then his hands are gone. I catch up on oxygen intake.

There's a rip of the plastic packet. He's opening a condom. The sound of latex against skin as he rolls it on. Then a slurping and I imagine him slicking his cock in lube, stroking until it glistens. My cunt clenches. I only have to think of his cock and I want it inside my tight butthole.

'I'll look after you, Sam. Just yell and I'll stop.'

'Shut up and fuck me, Coop.' Okay, it's not my best invitation but I'm far beyond polite.

I press back, adjust the hold on my buttocks so I'm pulling them wide apart, dying to feel his cock against me, inside me. Eager to seesaw between pleasure and pain.

A touch of wetness, and then the pressure of his hard thick cock pushing at the tight hole of my arse. The pressure increases. My body tenses, involuntarily trying to keep his cock out. I moan from deep in my gut, a rippling sound of need. There's the tiniest hint of give. A loosening, a relaxing. Thankfully he doesn't remove any pressure. I pant. More give. More pressure.

And then it slips inside. It can't be far because a burning squeeze is all I feel. He pushes in further and it's like I'm going to tear apart. In a good way. Burning pain. A deep aching throb. *Holy fuck.* Just as I'm about to scream because the pressure is almost too much, muscles relax and his cock slips further inside. My breath exhales in a groan that sounds a lot like 'Yes'.

His deep groan comes first, before his hands clench my buttocks. I grab hold of pillows. He has control.

As my butt relaxes, his cock slips deeper. It's an effort to hold still, for me anyway. I'm full of him and the pleasure is huge but with my panting, each breath is difficult to take as tiny jabs of sharp pain lance me with each tiny movement.

He's frozen and I'm worried the tight clench of my arse is hurting him. 'Are you okay?' I manage to puff out the question.

'You're so tight. It's like heaven. Fuck, Sam.' He sinks deeper inside me and this time it's all pleasure.

There's no more chatter as the rest of his cock slides inside, access assisted by his hand finding my clit and soaking, empty hole. A finger inside me, another on my clit. A long shattering moan is all I can give to show my appreciation.

A couple of deeply sucked breaths and I rock on his hand, pushing back on his cock. My muscles have eased, accustomed to the penetration. I need to move. I want Cooper spearing inside me.

'Sam. No.' The sharp edge to his voice has me pause but before I can work out what he wants, his voice strokes across every nerve ending in my back. 'I need to move.'

'Go hard, Coop.' It's all pleasure from here, I hope. There's more pleasure than pain filling me but it's so long since I've done this, I forget if it gets worse again. I know it gets better.

There's a giant pause, as if Cooper's nervous, or taking care not to hurt me. My heart skips a beat. Then his cock eases out, not fully, before thrusting in. Fast. My heart's racing. There's a tightening, followed by a sharpness I can't really call pain. It's an edge added to pleasure.

As he keeps moving the edge sharpens and the pleasure intensifies. Each movement, each stroke, each thrust adds and sharpens.

His groans become growls, each deeper and more guttural. The thrusts are faster, his fingers on my clit are hard, those inside me dig deep. Every nerve ending sings. Every muscle quivers. I'm hovering over the greatest orgasm that won't quite sweep me up yet.

'God, you're so tight.' He thrusts deep into my arse while pressing against my clit and I'm suddenly pushed over the edge. Muscles clench and release. My throat opens and a cry fills the room. I've never made a noise like it. Part scream, part shout, part ecstasy. It pushes me further, sends me higher, and I feel the tight clench around his cock. The tightening of my buttocks, the tension in my thighs.

'Shit.' Cooper's hips rock, his cock thrusting in and out with short sharp jabs. And then he slams hard against me, his hands clenched tightly on both my hips, pulling me harder to him. His body wraps around mine and I know he's experiencing the same depth of orgasm as I did. He's with me. Shaken and stirred. Soaring in the stratosphere. Flying. Flying until we land.

As my thumping heart slows, I can feel his heart beating the same rhythm as mine. His breathing matches mine.

His cock moves inside before pulling free. A deep shudder surges through me as he leaves. 'Ooohhh.' It escapes like an exhalation.

He removes the condom and drops it into the bin beside the bed before bundling me against him and curling around me.

'Are you okay?' His breath ruffles my hair and warms my ear.

'Yes.' But I'm not okay. Okay is too blah a word to describe how I am. 'No.' I hesitate and Cooper hugs me tighter. I'm quick to reassure him. 'I'm super. Incredible. Amazing.'

He kisses the edge of my ear. 'But it hurt?'

'Hurt good.' I'm struggling to form words, sentences. I can't formulate thoughts. It's like I'm still someplace celestial.

The warmth of Cooper's body encourages muscles to relax and I fall against him, knowing he'll hold me and keep me safe.

He gives a growl of satisfaction before our kiss halts the conversation. For the first time, the kiss doesn't heat me to fever point, even though it remains at our usual excellent standard. I'm sated. For now.

When we break, I run my fingertips over his chest, stroking mindlessly. Parts of my brain begin to function. Body parts commence loud communication with my mind. Before I can sort and verbalise, my stomach grumbles so loudly there's no need for words.

We laugh.

'How late is it?'

'Too late for chowder. Will room service do?'

We order. I should get up and shower but I can't be bothered moving.

Cooper sprawls on the bed beside me, one arm flung over his face. 'Sam.' He hesitates and I murmur to show I'm listening even if I can't move. 'I've ... I mean ... It's ... No ... Geez...' He stops and I wait. After too long, I wriggle up and lean over his covered face. It's a bit hard to see but I think his eyes are squeezed shut, his forehead scrunched and his jaw clenched. I run my thumb across his bottom lip. Back and forth. Then drop it to his chin, where I stroke his jaw.

Something's bothering him. And maybe I can guess, but if I get it wrong I'll be a total git. I aim for a conversation mid-ground, so I make less of a fool of myself if I'm wrong.

'Anal sex is raw, harsh, primal, illicit, dark and dirty. It gets me off so much more than normal sex. Did you feel like that?' I hold my breath hoping I've picked the right tack. If I'm wrong, what else could it be?

He could have hated it. He could have been hurt. And I didn't even think to ask. God, what kind of an idiot am I? How hard is it to say, 'Are you okay?' after he asks if I'm okay? I curse myself as all kinds of a fool. A selfish pleasure slut.

Chapter 10

Cooper rolls out of bed and walks into the bathroom. I either waited too long to find out what he wanted to say, or picked the wrong words.

I suck at this side of relationships. I have no idea how long to wait, how far to push, how much to share, how much to keep in reserve. I'm an action girl.

I curse under my breath. *Now what do I do?*

The bathroom door opens. Cooper's head appears with a cloud of steam. 'You coming in?' He lifts his brows. A bone-melting smile softens his face. 'I'm running a bath.'

I roll onto my side. 'With bubbles?'

'Of course. I didn't think you'd move without a lure.'

My legs slip off the bed and I make my way to the bathroom. The lure of Cooper would have been enough ... but I won't tell him that.

The bathroom is filled with steam and the scent of lavender. Bubbles fall over the edge of the bathtub. Cooper stands gloriously naked. What more of an invitation does a girl need?

Placing my hand into his outstretched one, he helps me into the bubble-bliss. Warmth envelopes my feet and lower legs. Foam whispers against my knees. I sink down as bubbles, like moist air, caress my skin all the way up to my neck. Warm water encircles, soothes, relaxes and hugs.

'Are you joining me?' My hand is still clasped with his so I give it a tug.

Cooper slides in behind me, legs around mine, arms circling my waist. I lean against the solid wall of his chest, making his shoulder my pillow. He nips my earlobe. A sharp sting of pleasure.

'I don't think I can explain how good that was. I've never experienced anything that hot,' he whispers against my ear. His hands slip and slide against me in a soothing manner, and I'm so sated that all I feel is relaxed.

'Hmmm.' I'd like to make a quip but my brain isn't up to it. Something about all our sex being hot, but I can't think how to word it. I'm not sure I can summon the energy to laugh, or even chuckle. You can't quip without at least a smile.

'Are you all done in, Sammy?'

I nod.

'You relax in the bubbles. I'll stop you drowning.' I know he smiles from the lifting of his cheek and the tensing of his hands. My body softens as I lean against him. I'm probably heavy but I'm too tired to worry.

We lie in silence, an easy companionable quiet. I drift off, held firmly on the muscle-pillow of Cooper.

When his foot moves and the resulting swirl of water brings goosebumps to my flesh, we stir. I squirm against the cold. A yawn escapes. I'm propelled to move. 'I have to get out, Coop, sorry but I'm cold.' Turning my head, he looks as sated and relaxed as I feel.

He presses a kiss to my lips. 'Dinner'll be here soon.' My raised eyebrows prompt his explanation. 'I asked them to bring it in an hour.'

It seems my earlier concerns were rubbish. He wasn't worried about the anal sex, just busy planning a bubbly seduction. I'm glad I didn't go for the pushy conversation. Maybe I don't suck at relationships, after all.

***

The morning light filters through the curtains, waking me. Last night we went from action to emotion. I've always been more comfortable with action, but with Cooper, it's different. Waking with him wrapped around me is no hardship, and today it brings extra surges of happiness, contentment and longing.

I've shared all I am and all that I have inside with him, and he's still here. The relationship problems I've had in the past don't exist with him, or the things that bothered others, don't bother him. He gives me hope. Hope that we could have a happy ever after with kids. But there's football. And I'm 38. It's all wrong.

Our timing sucks. If I wait for him to be ready, I'll be too old. But could I have a child without him?

I breathe slowly as a tiny ripple of nausea passes over me. Yesterday was full-blown panic. Today, just nausea. Maybe I'm improving and the clock won't tick out.

I stretch, slowly moving parts of my body away from his. It's akin to prying metal from a strong magnet. He stirs.

'Morning.' His smile is a deep and wondrous welcome. An invitation to the day. A gift of warmth and light.

'Hey. How did you sleep?'

'Like I'd died and gone to heaven. You?'

'Way too much.' I laugh before shaking my head. 'I feel stupid, Coop. I had you in the most divine bubble bath and I fell asleep on you. Then slept all night. I don't know where my stamina went.'

He lifts himself up on one elbow, his gaze intense, serious. It threatens my equilibrium.

'Sam, if you wanted anything to happen in those bubbles, you would've needed another bloke. The sex last night was so good I've not woken up raring to go for once. In case you hadn't noticed.'

Heat suffuses across my cheeks. I hadn't noticed. I hadn't thought about more sex yet, either.

'We don't have a dive until this afternoon. If you're tired, we could cancel.'

I squeeze his hand and shake my head. 'No. I'm not *that* tired. More sated than tired. So what will we do today?'

The hours disappear as we snorkel, swim, hike hills, take photos, talk, laugh and dive. As the sun is setting and we're walking back towards town, Cooper stops. I spin towards him, looking to see what's up. I know what he's thinking. We're in sync.

With gazes still in contact, we step closer together, our hands meet, fingers entwine. His eyes darken. Lips soften and bend upwards. His body bends slightly towards mine. His lips hover so close I could kiss them if I stretched but his breath touches my parted lips and I hesitate.

'I should shower before dinner.' His voice is husky and rich. 'And since you *need* to eat chowder...' He grins as he throws my words back at me. Heat pools between my thighs. I wish I hadn't been quite so adamant. My lips tingle, wanting to smile, wanting a kiss.

'I'll meet you there,' he says.

I'm trapped in the intensity of his gaze, the curl of his body towards mine, the deep timbre of his voice, and the thought of him showering. I should be used to him, used to this feeling, but it still rocks me. Still drowns me. Still has my heart thumping, stomach knotting, and moisture pooling south.

His free hand curls around my cheek, turning my face and tilting it upwards. He holds my cheek cupped in his palm, then he takes my bottom lip between his.

It's when he sucks on my lip, nestling it between his own, rubbing and exploring with the tip of his tongue, that's when I fall into him. When I moan. When I writhe against his body. That's when I know I am a woman in lust.

I'm just terrified it's the more fatal version, called love.

Before I make a complete spectacle, he releases my lip, sweeps across it with the flat of his tongue and winks.

'See you in 40 minutes at the chowder place?' The lift of his voice and eyebrow tells me he's checking it with me and so I nod, hopelessly incapable of anything more strenuous.

He jogs away and I watch. Lord almighty. His butt gets better each time I look at it. Tighter, more deliciously plump, swinging that rhythm of sex. And his legs. Yum. Thighs straining, hamstrings tight, calves bunched, tapered ankles. A T-shirt covers the muscles of his back but as his arms pump, his shoulders swing, biceps curl, forearms vein up, hands clench.

I can't believe I've been able to spend every moment with this hunk. I can't believe I've wanted to spend every moment with him.

I shake myself, physically and mentally. I have a dinner to prepare for.

After a shower, I apply lavish amounts of jojoba oil, the perfect moisturiser, all over. I walk through a mist of perfume. I swipe on mascara that I forgot I'd brought, and a touch of coral lipstick. I dig out white lace underwear and slip into a sky blue and yellow sundress. A shell necklace, strappy sandals and I'm set, with five minutes to spare.

When I get across the road, Cooper is three steps away and my breath stops at the same moment his feet do. Tan chinos, white shirt, hair wet but spiked up, wide grin. He's stunning.

A wolf-whistle splits the air.

But it's not my whistle.

'You look amazing, Sam.' The words come as he steps towards me and sweeps me into a hug.

But my hand on his chest stops him.

'Did you just wolf-whistle?'

That stomach-flipping, knee-shaking grin does its thing. Damn, I'm hopeless. I should be immune to it.

'Indeed I did.'

A frown burrows into my forehead. '*You* made a crass, rude wolf-whistle?'

He laughs. 'I learned from this sexy smart chick that sometimes it's more effective than words.' He grins and when I return the gesture, he sweeps in for a kiss. A quick one, thankfully. A mere brush of lips.

'I'm starving,' he says as he pulls away.

Hands wrapped together, bodies close, both laughing, we enter the restaurant. The waitress does a double-take upon seeing Cooper. The same waitress as before. Inwardly I roll my eyes. *Here we go again.*

She takes us to a table secreted in the corner of the restaurant where only a little candlelight and shadows disturb the privacy. We order two bowls of chowder right away; we don't need the menu.

'Enjoy your night,' she says politely to both of us.

Cooper rearranges the seating so he's closer, right beside me. He pours my water and hands me bread, keeping his thigh tightly pressed to mine. He eats with one hand so he can curl his fingers around my hand on the table. Inside I'm melting at the sweetness, secretly gloating at the public display of affection. I sip my water to hide my grin before Cooper can comment on it.

The waitress arrives with two steaming bowls of chowder. Carefully, she lays mine on the table before me, then with the same proficiency, places Cooper's down. After wishing us a good meal, and shooting the briefest dirty glance at me, she leaves. I guess a jealous look is better than my dinner landing in my lap. Inwardly I'm joyously grinning for me, and feeling the teeniest, tiniest bit of sympathy for the waitress. Cooper is everything she could possibly imagine.

Cooper leans over and presses a kiss to my mouth. A hard, passionate kiss that promises much but lasts only seconds. Grinning at each other, we dig into the chowder. Smooth broth. Sweet vegetables. Succulent seafood. A hint of salt with the thickness. Delicious.

And all the while a warm thigh rests against mine. A solid arm brushes mine. A smile is bestowed when I murmur my appreciation for the food, for Cooper allowing me to eat. A kiss is given when I break for bread. The evening is magical.

I'm eating the most divine chowder in the world, with the most divine man as my companion. I look up and we're alone. No waitress watching us eat. I smirk. The waitress knows now she has no chance with him.

My spoon rattles against the edge of the bowl when it drops suddenly from lifeless fingers.

'Sam?'

I jump as if guilty of something. And I am. I'm guilty of extra juicy thoughts taking me into the magical land of love, not lust.

'Sorry, just a runaway thought shocked me.' I laugh to cover my surprise at saying too much.

'What runaway thought?'

I shake my head but Cooper nudges me. He's laughing, joking with me. He probably thinks my mind is still in the bedroom; he has no idea I've wandered much, much further. I give a bit of a chuckle.

'Look at us.' I wave my hand at our closeness, the thigh contact, our bodies. 'When did we become a couple?' My question's asked with a laugh but I can hear the quiet hysteria that lies beneath. Are we a couple or am I delusional?

Cooper raises a brow but returns to his eating, still attached to me. 'Sometime between our last trip here and now.' He captures my look and grins. 'I think I might have asked for more than just a dive buddy. So it's all my fault.' His grin and chuckle send shivers along my spine. I remember. I'm a fuck buddy. Back to Lustland. It's not a difficult place to be.

I splutter as I shake my head, not in negative denial, but in an oh-I-can't-believe-you-said-that way. Then I watch him eat. I need the distraction to go back to Lustland. His lips part, the spoon slips in, he tastes, sucks, his lips close around the shiny metal. He opens his mouth and removes the spoon. His tongue flicks out to clean a drop of thick milky sauce. His eyes half-close as he chews then swallows. A tensing of his jaw, the dip of his Adam's apple. Another sweep across his lips with his tongue. Shudders run across my shoulder blades, causing me to squirm.

'Do I have something on my face?' His fingers touch his cheek, his lips.

I shake my head. 'Just thinking about dessert.' I grin suggestively.

'Thank God for that,' he mutters as he goes back to eating. I snort as I hold in a big laugh and turn my attention back to the chowder.

When I've scraped my bowl clean, Cooper's looking at me. 'Sure you got it all?' he asks. I smack his shoulder lightly so I don't hurt my hand but he still gets the message that he's a smart arse.

He leans close to me. I'm expecting a kiss but his lips move to my ear. 'What did you have in mind for dessert?'

My lips twitch as I run through the responses I could give.

'It's me you want, isn't it?' His voice is soft but I know he's laughing, teasing me. I nod. He flicks his tongue against the edge of my earlobe and I hold back a groan.

The waitress makes a throat-clearing noise as she comes to the table. 'I hope you enjoyed your meal,' she says as she clears the bowls. 'Can I get you anything else?'

'Just the bill, thanks.' I'm so together I shock myself. My voice sounds normal even with Cooper's mouth burrowing against my ear. I swat at his thigh playfully but he just tucks my fingers between his legs, murmuring in my ear about where he'd like my hand.

Laughing, I pull away from him and grab my purse to pay the bill.

'Where are you running to, Sam?'

'I'm paying, so I can get you somewhere private before we're arrested.' My answer's a hissed whisper but the muffled cough behind me indicates that at least the waitress heard, if not the rest of the restaurant.

I bite my lips together as I pay for our meal. It shouldn't be this funny. I should be more mature. Overtly passionate displays of affection are not something I like to see while I eat. I can't understand why I've found it so much fun as a participant when it's off-putting as a spectator.

A chuckle ripples up from inside. *Get a load of yourself. You're a fool.* As a spectator it's no damn fun—all watching, wishing, and no joining in. As a participant ... I look over at Cooper ... Lord, as a participant it's the best fun you can have.

Biting down my laughter, I nudge my chin towards the door. When I see Cooper stand up to walk out, I walk quickly outside, the laughter bursting from me as soon as I'm out the door.

'What's so funny?'

'Us. Look at us. We're like teenagers who can't keep their hands off one another.' I'm still laughing, choking the words out between snorts.

'And that's bad?'

I laugh again, tripping over my feet as I walk away from the restaurant and head towards the beach. I don't even ask if that's where we're going. 'It's just that I hate public displays of affection and here I am doing it. I don't know what's happened to me.'

'Me.' And he's gloating. One word says so very much and heats me to the core.

How we make it to the beach I'll never know. When you're wrapped around each other snogging, there is no way you should be able to negotiate walking too. Since we've been together all day every day, walking or running or swimming, I guess that's got our bodies in tune and our strides have matched to some degree.

Once our feet hit the sand we turn left towards the strip of grass and the rocks. Neither of us speak, but our bodies are discussing sex with moving hands, devouring lips. Stumbling along, hands stripping clothes from each other as we go, the cool air dances across my flesh.

'Are you cold?' Cooper wraps his arms around me and holds me still against him.

'No, not really. Just the air hitting me.'

'I love the way you respond to the slightest thing.' He runs the tip of his finger along my naked spine, making me arch into him. His finger rubs at the base of my back, slipping into the top of my butt crack and out. Sensuous. Sensual. Sexy.

'I love the way you touch me.' My words are muffled as my mouth slides across his collarbone, grazes his chest, latches onto his tight nipple.

We're on our knees, then on the ground, wrapped in each other, sandy grass scratching, moonlight allowing me to spy the intensity of his gaze as he touches me.

My hand wraps around his cock, stroking, teasing, squeezing. Little encouragement is needed for his hot, steely flesh. We're lying side by side, touching, staring, kissing, tasting, nipping, touching. A quick brush of lips changes to a kiss that consumes. My mouth meets his in a tangle of tongues and meshing of lips. Our breaths mingle. Moans of pleasure are indecipherable. I can't tell which sounds are mine and which belong to him.

Cool air brushes against my hottest flesh. My thigh rests across his hip. I rock closer to him and his cock nudges my heated core. I gasp, squirming away just a little even though his cock seems to chase me.

'We can't.' I've no idea where that came from. Surely I can't be stopping him?

'Why not?'

'No condom.'

Cooper stops still. The surf is loud. A bird mournfully cries. A whisper of wind rustles the leaves of the palm trees nearby. My body thrums, loudly. Louder than the surf but only I can hear it, thumping inside my ears.

'Sam, I always use condoms and I know you do too.'

I nod.

He makes a noise like he's clearing his throat. 'I should have talked to you before we got to this.'

'Talk to me? About what?'

'I think you'd make a great mother—'

I scramble off him so quickly I'm sure he's no idea where his words went or why he stopped speaking.

'No. No. No.' I grab at my clothes, shoving my dress on with no care as to how it looks. I just want clothes on and to be away. 'You're freaking me out.' I scrabble to my feet and try to walk away but he grasps my ankle.

'Sam. Stop.'

'No. No way.' I pull my foot free then spin to stare at him. 'I make decisions for me. I make decisions for my body. I do not get caught up in the moment. I am not falling for a fairy tale. I'm stronger than that. I'm in charge.' When I started speaking, I was strong, sure, certain. By the time I get to the last three words, I'm choking back a scream. Sucking in sobs.

I choke and flee.

I know I thought of having his child alone but it was just a thought. I didn't bloody decide. Now Cooper's gone totally and completely freaking insane.

I stop as if I've run into a tree but there's nothing there. Only a hiccup from me breaks the quiet.

And then footsteps, running. Cooper coming after me.

I can run, or I can stand and work this out.

I don't need long to decide. I turn back and walk towards Cooper. He doesn't deserve my flight, again.

'Geez, Sam. Sorry. I didn't mean to freak you out.' He captures my hand, still a few feet from me, and I wonder if he's too scared to come close, or too embarrassed to bundle me against him, or if he's realised we've had our time.

'You can't just make a decision like that.'

'You're right. I can't. I needed to talk to you first.' We stand there, looking at the ground, our feet, our joined hands, anything but at each other.

I have to sort this out and I can't do it standing in the middle of the public beach, even if it is dark. I look at Cooper and muffle a gasp. Naked.

'Ah, you're not exactly dressed for the walk home,' I say.

'No. I wasn't thinking.'

I try not to raise my eyebrows, scoff or agree too loudly. I just squeeze his hand and we head back to the beach.

'Feel like a swim?' I can't think of anywhere to have a discussion like this. At least the water is relaxing and I'm beginning to associate Cooper with water after all the snorkelling, swimming and diving.

He waits for me to slip off my dress and then we walk to the water's edge and into the surf. The white tips of the waves stand out in the moonlight. We stride in, trails of phospholuminescence around us. Waist deep, I sink into the water and allow it to wrap me with comfort.

'Sorry, Sam. I didn't do that very well.' Cooper's hand brushes against my arm, stroking downwards from my shoulder to my wrist.

'I'm fucked at this stuff, Coop. It's not your fault.' I shrug and sparkles flash in water droplets. 'I know I said the other day I wanted a child, but I shocked myself saying that. I know I've also got no time to waste. My biological clock is almost all ticked out. But...' I shake my head, not sure how to say this, not sure what I'm saying. I touch my fingers against Cooper's cheek. 'I'm not sure I'm ready to give things up to have a kid.' I take a deep gulp and wish I was plunging into the ocean rather than into these words.

'Give yourself time, Sam. It's only been a few days since you said it. Take time to think it through.'

A great knot's formed in my throat and I fight against it. I can't swallow it. I cough to try to dislodge it but it's a phantasm and not a real blockage. Once I cough, I can't stop. I cough and cough. My hand to my mouth, the other at my throat, continuous coughing.

Cooper stands behind me, wrapping an arm around my waist while the other rubs circles over my shoulder blades, right where the blockage is growing. The warmth of his body soothes. The heel of his hand works tension from my back. My coughing subsides and he wraps both arms around me.

'Coop, I'm 38. If I'm not ready when my clock's this loud, I'm never going to be ready.'

'You verbalised it days ago and scared yourself. Then I just pushed you when I shouldn't have. Sorry.'

'But why? Why would you...' I wave my hand ineffectively as no better words come to me. 'Why would you say that, think that?'

He nuzzles against my nape, licking a trail along my spine, flicking at the back of my earlobe. 'I like you, Sam. I like you a lot.'

I need to be sure of what he's saying. My mind's a jumble of things and I don't want to take this the wrong way. I gulp a breath. 'Are you offering to give me a child?'

His head moves against mine. A nod. He wraps his arms tighter against me and I feel his cock firm against my buttocks. 'I'd give you more if I could, but I can't. Not just yet anyway.'

'You what?' I tear myself out of his arms and spin towards him. 'We've known each other just over a week!' Hands on his chest, my heart's thumping and his is keeping pace beneath my palm. I stare at him. Although there's only moonlight, I can see the intensity in his face. Whatever he's saying, he's sincere. Or at least he thinks he is, right at this moment.

He looks up to the sky and then back at me. A deep sigh escapes before he speaks. 'I've never met anyone like you. I'd give you the world but I'm committed to football for the next two years.'

I shake my head to show I still don't know what he's saying.

'But you'd give me a child, *your* child?' My question is a whisper and awe fills my tone.

'If that's what you wanted. Yes.'

God.

God!

I make a noise like a hysterical fool.

'What?' he asks. 'Are you okay? Have I freaked you out again?'

I make a shallow dive underwater and let the cool ocean take the heat out of my brain. I come up next to him, shaking my head.

'Tonight, up there eating dinner.' I wave towards the hill. 'The waitress, who was after you a week ago, was out of the picture. Last week she flirted with you. This week, she acknowledged that she had no chance. It hit me that we're ... together.'

'When you dropped your spoon?'

'Yeah.' I duck underwater again. I surface a little further from him. I still don't feel in control. 'I don't understand how I can be only just working out we're together, and you...' I'm lost for what to say. 'You...' I throw my hands in the air still struggling with this words-emotions thing. 'You're comparing us to your long-term football contract.'

Cooper gives a short burst of laughter.

'Come here.' He opens his arms wide and I wade towards him. 'You're the most confident woman I've ever met in most circumstances. But talk about more than a holiday fling and you're a basket case. Would it be so bad to be together?'

'I don't do relationships.' He gives me a sceptical look and I explain further. 'I have short flings. Nostrings sex. Surely you know what I mean?'

He presses a kiss to my forehead, my eyes, each cheek and then to my mouth. 'I know you're worth more than that, Sam.'

My hand against his cheek, I look into his eyes. 'Your offer is beautiful. The most gorgeous thing anyone's ever offered. I ... I'm sorry ... I just can't take you up on it.'

But I can't leave him either. My lips press against his in a gentle touch, hopefully conveying so much more than I'm capable of with speech. Our mouths nibble and taste, before deepening to a hunger I'm more familiar with. Gasping for breath, but unable to break apart, the kiss turns to a prelude to sex. Great sex. Like we've always shared.

When we break apart, he lifts me up, holding me tight against the solid wall of his chest. 'Want to head home and have sex with a condom?'

I smile and lean forward, speaking against his lips. 'Sounds less complicated. Something I can handle.' He swats my behind but his smile is all carnal need. I can definitely handle that.

Chapter 11

'If we only have two days of diving left, will we see if we can do a night dive tonight?' I ask Cooper as we're heading to the morning dive. I don't want there to be only a few days left but I have to face it. The holiday is coming to an end.

'Sounds like a plan.'

At the dive shack before our morning dive, we book in. Then I think about the number of dives we're doing.

'Have I got too many dives? I don't want to be flying home getting the bends.' Even though I smile and it's said light-heartedly, I am serious. Too many dives, too deep, and not enough time to get the nitrogen out of my bloodstream could mean trouble on the flight home.

The dive shop operator, Brian, frowns. 'When do you fly home?'

'Saturday.'

'Oh, you'll be fine. You only need 24 hours without diving. Your last dive is Wednesday night?' Brian asks.

'Yes. We're climbing the mountain on Thursday but I was worried about doing so many dives.'

'They're only shallow. The dives today are no more than 10 metres. And tomorrow's no more than 18 metres. We'll have a dive computer. There's no way I'll compromise safety.'

I nod, reassured.

'Haven't you climbed the mountain before?' Brian asks. I've been diving with his company every holiday, so I'm one of his regular holiday-makers.

I laugh and rest the flat of my hand on Cooper's chest. 'No. This time I've been coerced.'

Brian exchanges a look with Cooper. Some male bonding thing I guess.

'So where are we diving this morning?' I ask as more divers arrive. I don't want Cooper's coercion a topic for public discussion.

The morning and the afternoon dives are in the lagoon and filled with fish, a turtle, reef sharks, nudibranchs, lots of photos and a great dive buddy.

Quite a few divers hang around to check out our photos. A small cheer goes up. Cooper's photo has won. Again. The other divers are enjoying our rivalry and have been voting on the photos. Hard as I try, I still can't get a better photo than Cooper. If we pick the top ten photos, I may have four or five in there. But when we narrow it to the top three photos, I never get more than one.

'You're unbelievable, Coop.'

He gives that ultra-sexy grin and leans close, whispering so only I hear. 'Do you really want to win, Sam?'

A shiver slices along my spine. I meet his gaze, the air shifts, and our stares lock. Breathing becomes difficult. I can only manage shallow gasps. I know he's baiting me. He's teasing, not being outright mean, but it hits a nerve.

Damn it. Do I want to win? Each time I think of it, the baby thought flashes large and luminous in my mind. But winning shouldn't be about anything but the competition. A child is too important to be part of a game. I need to separate these thoughts, in my mind and Cooper's.

Cooper pokes me in the ribs, whispering with some concern, 'Come back to me, Sam.' His look gentles, his lips soften, his hands cup my shoulders. 'That's better.' He's coaxing as if I'm a skittish animal.

Gritting my teeth, I make a show of growling loud enough so everyone hears. 'I'll be back to beat you tomorrow.' It's a competition, I can compete with the best. There's a cheer before people leave.

Our photos are saved to a USB. We erase the memory cards on the cameras and hand them back. 'They'll be ready again tomorrow,' Brian says. 'Unless you want them tonight.'

We look at each other, eyebrows raised.

'What kind of flash do we need for night?' I ask.

We're given a quick lesson on the equipment for night photography. The gear is all available for hire. 'Let's do it.' Cooper's enthusiasm is difficult to resist.

'You're on.' I high-five him. 'And may the best photo win.'

We leave to grab dinner before coming back for the night dive. Cooper's hand wraps around mine as we're walking. 'Sorry I baited you back there. I wasn't thinking.'

I shrug. There's nothing I can say. He knows my weakness and he exploits it. It's part of the competitive spirit. I knew it would be like this when I bared myself. Nothing I can say, or do. And he could be a whole lot nastier. 'I know you're competitive. I expected some stick from you. I'll survive.'

His fingers thread between mine, his palm against mine, holding me close. We walk in silence but it's not uncomfortable, or not terribly so. With a bit of a rueful smile, I glance across at him from the corner of my eye. His jaw's clenched, his eyes half open, and his forehead's creased.

I'm not getting through to him. 'You exploited my weakness, it's what competitors do. But our competition isn't about a baby. We both know that. Our competition is between us. The baby issue is completely separate.'

He nods. 'I was playing dirty and I don't usually do that. Sorry.' He looks shattered.

I lean close and skim my hands up his chest, over those deliciously huge shoulders and up to cup his jaw. I flick my tongue across his bottom lip. His absent smile concerns me. The worry etched into his face, with fine lines around his eyes and mouth, has me sliding my fingers across the marks, smoothing his skin.

'Just don't do it again.' If he's this concerned, he never will.

I wriggle my hips against his groin and close my lips over his. His mouth meets mine. Hot, hard and hasty. My hands slip behind his head, one curved around his skull, the other teasing his nape. My hips are confined by his hands, held still, pushed tight against his thick cock.

A muffled laugh, then a voice breaks through the kiss-fog. 'I thought you two were grabbing a quick dinner?'

Our kiss breaks but our body contact remains. 'Doesn't this count?' I ask. Brian shakes his head, laughing as he cycles away.

Cooper shuffles my hips away from his but our hands remain holding tight. 'We'd better eat. He won't wait for us now he knows why we're late.'

We eat and are back at the dive shack before the other divers, but not before Brian.

'Please tell me you ate more than each other's tonsils.' He's grinning like we're back in high school and we're 15-year-olds caught pashing. Then he laughs and waves his hand towards the front door. 'I think I'm gonna call it "The Love Shack", what do you reckon?' He chuckles at his own joke but, fortunately for us, becomes busy with the crowd arriving.

The night dive has 10 on it, which is a fair size group for the night. Cooper and I have our gear from earlier today, we just need refilled air cylinders. We gear up quickly and then go through the camera equipment we've hired, familiarising ourselves with the flashes and strobes.

'Have you done night photos before?' I ask Cooper.

'Nope. You?'

I shake my head.

'So, level playing field.'

I scoff. 'Hardly. You're streets ahead of me.'

He looks at me with the boyishness from a week ago, not the haunted look from an hour ago, and my chest swells.

Before I can say anything more, we're called to load up. I brush my fingers across Cooper's and then fill my hands with equipment and walk to the boat.

The night dive is amazing. Three sleepy turtles make great photographic subjects. A couple of reef sharks, like puppy dogs, follow us around. Slumbering schools of fish hide amongst weeds or behind rocks. Shadows darken and decorate. Cooper and I jostle light-heartedly for photos. I set off my strobe light a couple of times hoping to overexpose his pictures. Not the nicest thing to do but I don't think I've any hope of winning without resorting to some tricks, and he's a good sport.

Lugging the extra lighting and laughing must use up a lot more air because the dive goes quickly. When we're heading back to the exit point, I take a quick snap of Cooper and his three guard sharks. There's something about the shadows, the bubbles and the intensity of Cooper's gaze that makes me snap it for a memento.

Before making our ascent, Cooper does an elaborate mime which leaves me snorting bubbles and sucking air as laughter erupts. He wants me to pose as a pole dancer on the anchor line. I strike a few poses but pole dancing with scuba and camera gear isn't something I imagine will take off.

When we reach the surface, I'm still spluttering, almost unable to lift the camera and lights out of the water.

'It's not that funny, Sam.' Cooper helps with lifting the gear out before holding my waist while I struggle with my fins.

'It's ridiculous. The whole idea is insane. The photos will be crazy.'

'More photos?' asks one of the other divers.

'Yes, but you don't need to wait around for these ones.' I don't want people seeing my pole dancing. It was silly enough in private.

'Oh, no, we'll be waiting. Some of the divers from today told us about your contest. They're coming back tonight to see the next lot of photos and vote.'

'What?' The tension in my voice makes the pitch increase to a level I'm not pleased about. It's at crazy fish-wife level.

The laughter among the divers is loud and the discussions about us become fierce. Cooper helps me out of the water while I'm inwardly blustering.

'When did this become a public vote? I thought this was between us.' I'm ranting but I can't stop myself. I struggle out of the dive gear, stand the air cylinder in the rack and start packing up with short sharp movements.

'It gives people enjoyment, Sam. Don't sweat it. They don't know it's anything more than a bit of fun.'

I glare at him.

'People like us are rare, Sam. You know that. We compete hard but remain friends. It intrigues others. And they want to be involved in something, even if it's only a minor role. They're sports fans cheering us on. No more. You can cope with that. I know you can.'

That's the trouble. I don't know that I can. Triathlon isn't a sport that attracts major fans, not like football. Cooper might be used to this sort of public involvement in his life but I'm not. I'm scared of being judged and found wanting.

Did I just think that?

Sighing deeply I muster up my courage. 'You're right. It's a bit of fun. Sorry I lost perspective.'

We return to shore, clean and pack up, and then go into the dive shack for the camera download.

'What the...?' Cooper's hand squeezes my shoulder when I stop in the doorway. There must be 20 people jammed into the room.

The conversations stop and a low hum of anticipation fills the air. Oxygen expels through my lips, even with my jaw clenched. Cooper gives another squeeze.

'Here they are, our competitors, Sam and Cooper.' Brian makes an announcement like we're royalty entering a ball. I shake my head and laugh. There's not a lot else to do.

We both hand over the cameras and step back to see how the shots have gone. I'm jostled as others crowd in. It's the craziest thing I've ever seen. People cheering photos by amateurs.

My photos are downloaded and then Cooper's but we don't get to check them out first. They're going to make a slideshow so everyone can see. *Brilliant. Public anchor dancing. Can't wait for that.*

The photos are loaded and a hush falls over the crowd. A couple of nice shots of turtles snoozing. A couple of flash flares ruin some ordinary shots and Cooper gives me a smirk, as if to say he knew I was trying to ruin his shots and took poor ones on purpose. Cooper has a brilliant shot of shadowed seaweed and rock. And then another of shadowed sand and ripples. He's made great use of the shadows and I raise my eyebrows and tip my head to him. He has an excellent eye for lighting.

Cooper's photos finish off with a bunch of incredibly stupid but well-composed shots. They're like the ice breakers at a party. The snaps that make people laugh. I'll never make a pole dancer, I look much too uncomfortable. But they are fun shots and Cooper has a good eye for an angle.

More okay photos from my camera. I have a nice one of a school of sleeping fish. Then the next photo has my breath catch. Not only my breath; there's a simultaneous gasp in the room. It's the photo I snapped quickly, on a whim, and it's stunning. Eight pairs of dark, shiny eyes peer from shadows, cast in a flare of illumination. The noses of the three sharks gleam, as does the edge of the mask and regulator on Cooper's face. It could be on black and white film. It's hauntingly beautiful.

While I'm trying to catch my breath, applause breaks out.

I've always heard it said that sharks have deadly flat eyes with a predatory gleam but these sharks don't. These sharks look like they're smiling, their eyes dark and shiny. The human has the gaze that sends prickles down my spine. A hungry, predatory gleam is in Cooper's eyes, for everyone to see. I could kick myself. I don't want just anyone to see that gaze, to recognise that stare.

I look at Cooper, desperately wishing I could apologise for showing his hunger to the world, but he's laughing. There's no resentment, only amusement and happiness. He captures my glance and bows, blowing me a kiss. I frown, but nod, not really sure what he's trying to convey. Maybe he doesn't see what I do in the photo.

The photo makes me feel hollow but no one else seems to be concerned. They're all laughing and cheering, like it's a brilliant shot.

The slideshow is done and a chant starts up around the room. It takes me a while to work out what they're saying.

'Eyes' is the chant.

It's a long minute before I work out that my photo has won.

The eyes photo appears back on the screen and a cheer goes up. Three sharks and the giant predator with the hungry gaze. My heart races. I look over at Cooper and he's grinning, seemingly unaffected by his raw hunger caught in pixels. Brian grabs my wrist and lifts my arm in victory.

'Finally, Sam gets a win. Three cheers for Sam.' The cheering is loud, as are the congratulations and the back-slapping. Through it all I keep looking at Cooper. He sneaks glances at me. We smile at each other, a quiet communication in the chaos that ensues.

I thought we'd kept to ourselves the last week or so. Lost in our own private world. But it seems we've made a lot of acquaintances with the divers at Lord Howe. Most are holiday-makers, like us, passing through. The few words exchanged before or after a dive have apparently confirmed a friendship. And that's kind of true. Holiday friendships are easy, brought about by a mutual interest, and gone during the trip home. In other years I've had similar experiences when I've struck up holiday acquaintances with divers. This time is different. My friendship with Cooper has eclipsed all other meetings. My conversations with him have overshadowed any other conversation.

I hadn't realised.

Or have I only pretended not to realise how close we've become?

I lose the thread of the conversation around me. There's a momentary panic within me as I try to decipher these observations. If this friendship has eclipsed all others, what does that mean? Does this still end on the trip home? I can't work it out now. It's too noisy and the questions too hard.

Thirty minutes later, most people have left. Brian adds tonight's photos to our USB sticks.

'You guys have been great for business,' he says. 'Want to book in for next year now?'

Cooper laughs and I shake my head.

Brian grins and nudges Cooper. 'Take her home.'

I protest but not strenuously. I've been waiting for Cooper to take me home. I have a little bit of pole dancing I need to practise—with no wetsuit, no scuba gear, no cameras but plenty of wet, wanting, willing woman.

Chapter 12

The next day, after the double dive out at the Admiralty Islands, with lunch on Neds Beach, we arrive at the dive shack to another crowd with hot drinks and nibblies. We don't get more than four steps off the boat before hands reach for the cameras. Brian grins and says, 'We thought we'd have a bit of a party for the last showdown. Some mainland news guy's here too.'

The news guy aims straight for Cooper, armed with a notebook and asks for an autograph. No hello. No how are you. No do you mind. Then he shoots a photo of Cooper while he signs. When Cooper hands him back the notebook, he launches into questions about Coop's holiday, the dives and his photography. He finishes off with, 'I'll catch you inside,' before he whirls away. Cooper hardly says a thing worth reporting.

As we walk up the beach to clean and drop off the gear, I turn to Cooper. 'This is insane.'

He catches hold of my fingers. 'You really aren't used to the public spotlight, are you?'

'You mean this isn't odd—the autograph, the reporter?' My eyes widen and I frown as I try to work out if he's serious.

'Not entirely.' He shakes his head a little. I keep staring at him. 'People think they know you, that they're friends with you. Didn't that happen to you?'

I laugh. 'Good God, no.' Doesn't he realise that crowds don't follow triathlons? 'So, even though you play league in AFL territory, people still know you, you still have fans?'

He twists his mouth in something between a smile and a grimace. 'Yeah.'

'And this...' I wave my hand towards the dive shack. 'This public involvement in our ... our private business, doesn't shock you?'

He gives a short bark of laughter that contains no amusement. 'Not any more. It used to.' He hesitates as if thinking back in time. 'It used to bother me until I learned you can't change it, or control it, you can only roll with it.'

'So how do you get any privacy?'

'They're sharing a tiny part of me. I control how much more is shared, and usually that's minimal.'

I must show my doubts because he moves closer and wraps his arm across my shoulder, his lips touch my ear. 'They know we're competing. That's it. They don't know how much we compete, or what we mean to each other.'

I nod, slide my hand across his stomach and hang on to his waist.

He nips my ear. 'Give away only what you want to. Protect yourself.'

What we mean to each other. Hell? What's that? It's more than friendship. It's deeper than a fling. I don't want to go there. Not here. Not now.

I squeeze his waist. 'Thank you.' Sometimes Cooper's quiet self-assurance and generosity shake me to the core. It shouldn't. They're two qualities I love about him. Each time I experience them, my heart swells. That he shares them with me is incredible.

I turn my head and press a quick kiss to the corner of his mouth. I can't find the right words to express myself verbally and I hope my kiss expresses enough. Humour is so much easier and stops my wayward thoughts. 'Let's go see if I can beat you ... again.' I give his waist one last touch as I turn back towards the crowd.

This time there's a big screen slideshow and that brings me to a halt at the doorway, but Cooper's hand low on my spine reminds me I need a backbone to get through this.

Pulling in a deep breath helps me find my courage. A cup of tea is shoved into my hand and a plate of fruit cake into the other. Brian has a seat for Cooper and me at the back near him and the computer.

'Big show,' Cooper says.

'Hope you don't mind but it's the best fun we've had in ages. Two tough competitors leaving nothing to chance.'

I do a crazy eye roll but Brian only laughs and digs his elbow in my side. 'Next time you bring a big name to town, Sam, warn me beforehand and we'll put on something better than this.'

I say nothing, just give what I hope is an enigmatic smile. This fame Cooper deals with easily is confronting. I imagine it's worse for him in Melbourne and that makes me feel ill.

Cooper gives me a surreptitious wink.

The photos begin. Cooper's are first today. He has some great shots of fish and a brilliant one of seaweed brushing a colourful nudibranch. There appears to be movement in the shot. It's magical. I can't give him my opinion because the room is full of loud critique. I blow him a tiny kiss. He nods. He thinks he's won.

My photos come up. Most are ordinary. My first dive didn't inspire photographic greatness. I couldn't get a good shot in my mind, let alone find one in reality. Right at the end of the first dive I took a fantastic shot and it comes up on screen now. Another collective gasp makes my lips push out a smile. I moved to macro mode and took some funny shots. This one is a close up of a brightly-coloured wrasse's mouth and eye. The colours jump from the screen.

It was a lucky shot. You can't organise for those guys to come close.

The room is filled with silence as the rest of my shots pop on screen. I've played with lighting and macro settings and the photos have worked. I'm incredibly pleased, almost to the point of preening. There are fish, unusual angles of rocks, tiny shells, nudibranchs, little weeds, a miniscule pile of rubble, and Cooper, of course.

I look over at the subject and he's immobile. His face is blank, staring straight ahead, and I wonder if he's seeing the images on screen and cringing inside at my obvious adoration, or if something else is on his mind. The news guy is glued to his side.

I'm still puzzling about him when a thunderous cheer goes up and my close up of the fish is declared the winner.

Cooper laughs loudly. 'I've been beaten by a mouth.' He tilts his head and congratulates me.

For the next half hour or so, a slideshow of all our photos is projected on the screen while people mingle and chat. I'm caught with people I've seen on dives but not spoken more than a few words to. Cooper's right, people do think they know you. I fob off questions that are almost intimate, stunned they think I might give personal details. Although maybe they don't expect an answer because they don't push to receive one, just move on to the next topic or the next person. The reporter never comes near me but he hovers around Cooper all night. Obviously a fan.

Brian booms before the crowd breaks up, asking people to vote for an overall winning photograph. To make it easy, he has our six daily winning photos, four of Cooper's and two of mine, which he plays on a continuous loop. They're great photos and I can't pick which is best. I love the sharks but mostly for the look in Cooper's eyes. His firefish will most likely win.

The clinking of a spoon against a glass brings the room to silence. Brian gives a little speech thanking everyone for their votes and support, but making a big deal of thanking us for our competition. The room cheers. 'The winner of the best overall photo, by popular opinion is...' Brian draws it out. I'm not nervous. I don't think I have a chance of winning. I'm looking at Cooper across the room and a ghost of a smile flickers across his lips when he captures my look, but it's gone quickly. The reporter glances up to follow his gaze but before he can connect the look to me, a photo flicks onto the screen.

The sharks.

My stomach goes into freefall.

I blink. Look again. It's still my photo.

'Sam, congratulations.' Brian hands me a small box of Lord Howe Island coasters. 'Please accept a small memento of your win.'

I'm wrapped in a hug from Brian. Then a heap of back-patting and hand-shaking. A huge grin from Cooper and a wave is all he can manage, crowded in as he is.

I've won.

I've beaten Cooper.

With a fluke of a photo but who cares? No one knows I took it on a whim, at the last moment. As a memento of my lust.

It takes an age before most of the crowd depart. I spend a few moments thanking Brian for looking after me again before I make my way outside. Cooper's still caught up with his crowd, so I shoot him a look across the room as I leave. I hope he understands I'm escaping and I'll see him outside.

I wander down to the water's edge and stare into the distance until my eyes ache. Meeting Cooper has stirred up so much inside me that I can't make sense of how I feel. I love being with him. I love competing with him. It's a thrill whether I lose or win.

But will I see him after the holiday? Or, maybe the better question is, do I want to? I hesitate and a small grin works its way onto my face. *Hell, yes.* He's the best sex I've ever had. This is the best holiday I've ever been on, because of spending time with him. I'd love to see him again.

Could we have a successful relationship full time? I don't know. Do I want a child? Do I want his child? Do I want his child without him around?

So many questions and no answers. The night is cooling off and Cooper could be caught for ages. I head slowly towards town, splashing in the shallows, trying to distract my thoughts. Before long there's the sound of someone running behind me. It makes me grin. Cooper catches me around my waist with a whoop as he slows beside me.

'Did you survive, Sammy?' His enthusiasm's infectious and my solemn mood lifts instantly. I've become a competitor again.

'Yes.' I hesitate for a second and then crow, 'Because I won.' I can't help laughing while I gloat. All thoughts of any rewards are left behind for this moment of pure pleasure. I won.

'I hate to tell you, but overall I'm still winning with the photos.'

I stop. 'How do you work that out?'

'Well, you've won the last two and the most popular, so that's three. I'd won four before that. So that means I've won, four to three.' He captures me, picks me up and holding me tight to his chest, spins us around. 'Don't go enjoying your winning streak too much.'

Laughing, I reply, 'I'll bask in my win, thank you very much.' I plant a quick kiss on his mouth. I can't argue with his logic, or his maths, but I'm still happy with my win. A win is a win, especially when competing with him.

He puts me back on my feet. Wrapped together, we make our way home. 'Why does your apartment feel like home?' I ask the question before my brain catches up. I want a baby, I don't. I want a relationship, I don't. I want Cooper, I ... Hell yeah. That's the only thing I do know. I'd want him with my last breath.

Cooper opens his mouth to speak, then his eyes flare. He shuts his mouth quickly and turns away.

I follow, silent until we get inside. 'What? What popped into your mind and stopped you speaking?'

'Nothing.' He stands in the bathroom and sheds his clothes. 'You joining me?' He turns the taps for the shower without waiting for my answer. He steps in under the steaming water and I can't help myself. I strip and join him.

Taking the soap, I rub it between my hands until suds fill my palms. I rub my hands across Cooper's chest and stomach. I lather up again and soap his arms and shoulders. Pressing a quick, open-mouthed kiss against his lips distracts me for only a moment. I move behind him and soap up his back and buttocks, before dropping to my knees and lathering his legs.

I even wash his feet, lifting each and soaping and rinsing.

My ministrations are sensual but quick. We're both conscious of not wasting water. Lord Howe Island relies on rainwater, having no rivers for supply, and we haven't had rain since we've been here.

Cooper takes the soap from me, stands me against him, stroking my back with suds and huge palms. He cups my buttocks and pulls me close. A squeeze and he releases me. His hands sweep along my arms, across my shoulders, down my breasts, over my stomach and between my thighs. I love his touch. His hands are certain, his touch smooth, his knowledge of my body insurmountable. From the moment he touches me I want to groan but his movements are so rapid the groan doesn't have time to build and expel.

When suds have gone and we're both clean, he holds me tight to his chest, face protected from the spray but water dropping all over me. Salty water gone from my hair, he reaches around and turns the water off.

I look up and his thumbs brush away droplets from my eyes. His lips close over mine. He tastes me at first, as if I'm an exquisite food for him to sample. His lips touch, move lightly, nibble, press firmly for a moment, before softening and sucking on mine. My knees weaken. I'm clinging to his shoulders and a sound not unlike a deep purr reverberates throughout the room.

Our kiss breaks. With an arm still wrapped over my shoulder blades, he walks me out of the shower and bundles me into one of the huge fluffy bath sheets. He holds me for a long time, making sure I find my feet back on the bathroom tiles, before he grabs a towel and roughly dries himself.

I love to watch.

I like the way the towel flicks over him, baring flesh then covering it. Water droplets shimmer before he brushes them away. His arm muscles flex as he moves. His tight buttocks have deep shadowed dips. I drool over the thick thigh muscles as he lifts his leg or bends.

I need to get another occupation.

'Are you done?' he asks, prompting me to briskly rub the towel over myself. When I'm finished, I rub my hair with the towel, getting rid of most of the water.

'Coop...' I say his name without being entirely sure what else I want to say. He murmurs. I have to say something more but I'm not even sure where to start. 'Thank you.' That will have to do.

'What for?'

I let out a big sigh. 'Everything. But mostly for getting me through tonight, for coping with my freakouts, for making this the best holiday I've ever had.'

'Sam.' Cooper strokes his thumb across my cheek and leaves it sitting against my lower lip. My lip throbs beneath his touch. 'It's been my absolute pleasure. No hardship at all. And definitely the best holiday I've ever had.' His thumb slides over my chin and he plops a quick kiss to my lips. 'But this isn't over.'

'I know. We've got the walk tomorrow, and Friday.'

He gives me a look that I can't interpret and his lips twitch before he gives a sharp chuckle. 'Us, Sam. We're not done.'

'We aren't? But how's that work when you're in Melbourne and I'm in Adelaide?'

'I don't know exactly but this is too good to give up.' He frowns, a hesitation before he says, 'Unless you don't find it like that?'

I take hold of his hand and kiss the back of his knuckles. 'Yeah, I find it like that. It's kind of scary though.'

'So long as we're both scared we can work it out.'

'I like your optimism.' I close my teeth around his big middle knuckle, biting sharply, before soothing with my tongue. 'Can we talk about this later? I've been waiting all day to have my wicked way with you.' I give a fake leer and swipe at the towel still wrapped around his waist.

'Sam, what we have is more than just sex. You know that, don't you?'

I meet his gaze. It's honest, clear, intense. It's not just me who's falling somewhere deeply out of their depth.

'Yeah, I know, but right now all I want is you writhing beneath me while we have more than just good sex.'

He chuckles, allowing me to once again get away with avoiding the deeper issues, and that's good because I don't know how to face the deeper stuff.

Chapter 13

I wake slowly from a sexy, hot dream only to find I'm not dreaming. I am sprawled across a sexy hot man whose hard cock nudges my thigh.

'Hey, Coop.' My sleepy murmur sounds thick and full of lust.

'Hey yourself.'

'I see my riding efforts last night haven't worn you out.'

Cooper gives a deep chuckle that rumbles from his chest right through my rib cage. Goosebumps spring up all over my skin. 'I'm sure it didn't wear you out either, Sammy. Not judging by those little sounds you were making while you woke.'

Ah, yes. Those little sounds. 'It was a pretty steamy dream.'

Cooper nuzzles beneath my jaw and his cock wriggles beside my thigh. 'Did it feature me?'

I chuckle. 'Well ... I'm not sure, you woke me too soon.'

Cooper grabs me and flips me onto my back, his mouth moving straight to my nipple and sucking tight before dragging it out as he releases. I make one of those little noises before locking my legs around his hips and squirming beneath him. 'Do we have time?'

'We have five minutes until breakfast is deliv—'

My arm flies out for a condom, which I rip open with my teeth. In record time I sheath his cock in latex and direct it inside me. Relief. And then he pounds into me.

Dear God. The little noises quickly become very loud sounds. And as I shout his name and cling to him, there's a knock on the door.

Breakfast.

I shouldn't laugh but I do. Cooper buries his head in my shoulder.

'I'll get it.' After I make the offer, he rolls away. I grab his gown and sash it around my waist, run my fingers through my hair and open the door to take the breakfast tray from the discreet room service lady who only blushes and refuses to meet my gaze.

When I come back he's grinning.

'Did they know what we were doing?'

A burst of laughter explodes from me. 'Oh, yeah. Sometimes I think the whole freaking island knows what we're doing.'

'You shouldn't be so loud.'

'You shouldn't be so good.'

We breakfast quickly, then jog down to meet the group for the mountain walk. The groups are limited in size but ours is even smaller than the maximum, with us, two older couples, and the guide.

We introduce ourselves. Jim and Sue are one couple, Matt and Margaret the other. Greg is the guide.

Jim looks when Cooper introduces himself. 'You look like that bloke ... plays for Melb—'

'Yeah, I get that all the time,' Cooper says with a grin.

'So what do you do for a crust?' Matt asks.

Cooper looks at me, so I answer. 'I'm a children's sports coach.'

Sue gapes. 'I don't think I'm fit enough for this walk.' Her voice is above a whisper but there's a quiet desperation in it.

'You'll be fine,' Greg says. 'You've done lots of walks harder than this. We talked about it earlier.'

'I coach kids, Sue, to run, swim and ride. I don't do a lot of bushwalking and these hills are bigger than I'm used to.' I smile gently, hoping to reassure her. There's nothing worse than defeating yourself mentally before you start.

I glance at Cooper. I need to listen to my own advice. My aversion to relationships and children may be defeating me before I start.

Sue nods her thanks. 'Where are you from?'

'I'm from Adelaide, you?'

'We're all from Sydney.'

There's a lull in the conversation before Matt takes up the unanswered question. 'What did you say you did, Cooper?'

Cooper's smile is reluctant and rueful but he answers the question. 'I play football.' When Jim does a double-take, Cooper smiles. 'Yeah, like you said, I look like him.'

'Oh my goodness.' Sue covers her mouth with her hand. 'We won't tell anyone you're here. It must be awful.'

Cooper brushes my arm lightly. 'It's okay. I'm used to it.' He might be, but I'm not.

Margaret looks from one of us to the other. She frowns up at her husband, obviously trying to convey something to him but he's not receiving. Eventually she says, 'I'm sorry, but it is league you're talking about and you're the Australian halfback?'

Cooper nods and I do a bit of my own double-take. *Australian halfback?* He downplayed that. In all the Olympics talk he didn't once offer that he too had represented the country.

Margaret frowns and swings her hand in the air between me and Cooper. 'But they don't play league in Adelaide, do they?'

The four men make that strained laugh men make when they're embarrassed. I answer her. 'Cooper and I aren't ... that is...' *Oh shit. What are we?* I take a breath and try again, conscious of the burning intensity of Cooper's gaze. I've jumped in too quickly and I've no idea what to say. I should have left this to him. I can't embarrass him. I can't straight-out lie. I don't want to tell the complete truth. *Hell.* I look up and meet Cooper's stare hoping to convey to him my difficulty in expressing us. He only smiles, leaving me to stammer, 'We only met recently. We've been diving together.'

A loud 'Oh' escapes the group. I'm not sure if that's 'Oh, our mistake, you're not together', or 'Oh, you don't want to tell us', or some other 'Oh'.

'We'd best be heading off.' And with that, Greg calls us all to attention and the walk begins.

I was hoping the group would split into couples and I'd be able to speak to Coop, but it splits by gender, and I'm left with Sue and Margaret. They are lovely and it's pleasant as we walk towards the base of the hills, chatting. But I keep zoning in on the men's conversation, trying to hear more about Cooper. They're talking football but it seems more generic than specific, and Coop's not saying much.

The walk is difficult for Sue and Margaret. It's single file, lots of vertical climbs with just a rope and your balance to hoist you up, and they're struggling. Although they're continuing without complaint. The conversation drops as the walk becomes a climb. A serious climb.

The vegetation is ever-changing. Thick and lush at places, stunted and struggling when exposed. Sometimes trees as far as you can see. Other times not a tree nearby and only small ferns and mosses struggling to hold to the precarious rock face. Big mountain palms break out from the top of the canopy whenever we get a view. It's incredible. A challenging walk but breathtakingly beautiful.

We reach the summit and it is spectacular. Worth every drop of sweat, every tired muscle. It's a stunted rainforest, suitable for hobbits and other fairy folk. Sue and Margaret are ecstatic to have made the effort. The ocean is endless blue with only the solid grey wall of Balls Pyramid jutting from the deep to disturb it. Lord Howe Island, a gleaming emerald, is spread beneath us. Lots of thick vegetation, with tiny strips of flat pasture land. Incredibly beautiful. We're so lucky to be here. The hills at the far end of the island look miniscule, and Malabar Hill is not miniscule as my legs well know.

The sky is dazzling azure without a cloud to be seen, which is fortunate because if there were clouds they would no doubt be around the mountain hiding this stunning vista. A cloudy mist hangs in the forest and in each dip in the mountainside.

The lagoon is still. Every shade of blue and green on display—turquoise, emerald, lime, azure, navy, teal, periwinkle, dark olive, and sea green. The patches of coral are dark, the holes we've dived even darker. Beyond the lagoon, the ocean stops at the edge with precision in white foam. There's churning and deeper colours and shades where the ocean floor dips and hollows.

After we've gasped and filled the air with oohhs and aahhs, we find a spot for lunch. Another group affair. There hasn't been time for individual discussions, so I've not been able to talk to Cooper about my growing discomfort. There's something about the men that bothers me. It prickles my unease. I can't put my finger on exactly what it is. I spend lunch time watching and listening. If I think on the way down, I might work it out.

Jim talks a lot through lunch. His kids have begun adult lives and he's full of talk about them. I'm glad I haven't been with him for most of the climb. He gets on my nerves with his endless chatter and bragging.

He draws a breath and looks at Cooper. 'You moved across the country when you were a kid. Your family's in Queensland, aren't they? I don't suppose you see them very often.'

I stare at Jim, then at Cooper, back to Jim. *Does everyone know everything about him?*

'Yes, I grew up in Queensland, and no, I don't get back there much.'

I watch Cooper as he speaks. His words are quiet, delivered simply, but there's unease about him I haven't seen before. His eyes don't quite meet anyone's. His shoulders are drawn back tightly. And his smiles have disappeared. This is a Cooper I haven't met before and one I'm not sure how to reach. And he hasn't talked. He just rephrased what was told to him. That's weird. Not like Cooper with me at all. They seem to know *about* him, and I know him. I think, although it makes me wonder.

Once lunch is over, we retrace our steps. It's almost silent and definitely awe-inspiring. There's more time to look and listen on the descent. The occasional bird swoop and bleat, a discordant noise, tears the stillness. The ocean below hisses against rocks in a rhythm as soothing as a sighing breeze. Chatter is minimal. I'm not sure if it's because the older couples require their breath or if the majesty of the place has captured and silenced them.

I stand near Cooper at one tight corner where we've stopped for a break and I slip my fingers into his hand, squeezing and giving him a smile when he looks at me. He smiles back but it's tight and strained. I trace my thumb across the back of his hand, stroking over muscle and veiny outcrops but he doesn't relax. The walk continues.

We head back to earth, and the path is slower going on the downhill journey. It's steep and somewhat slippery. At certain points, Greg and Cooper help everyone across.

Cooper naturally helps everyone. He's unassuming, polite, but always there. Not once has someone needed assistance and he hasn't been on hand to provide it. Even the simplest action of touching an elbow to steady Margaret, or holding out a hand to give Sue the confidence to jump a small opening.

As I watch him, my heart swells. The dive buddy I've had is real. He hasn't invented this kindness, this consideration. It's truly him.

I understand him better after today. I had no comprehension of his fame, for want of another word, but seeing the men 'own' him within seconds of meeting him has stunned me. The way Jim knew about Cooper's family, and assumed he knew him, is frightening.

I shiver.

'Cold, Sam?' Cooper's voice is a soft rumble from behind me.

I shake my head. 'No, sorry. Just thinking.'

'Whatever it is can't be good.'

I bite my lips together and shake my head. I know he can't see my face but I don't want him to know how my thoughts have affected me. If I speak, I'm scared he'll hear my concern, my fear. I was beginning to think I could take a chance on him but I don't know that I can survive his fame.

We keep walking, almost in silence, until the path widens. Cooper comes up beside me and our arms brush against each other. I turn and smile, ready to catch his hand and talk about the trip but Jim stops ahead of us and turns back, asking Cooper more football questions and effectively taking my place beside Coop. Margaret and Sue are in front of us. Greg and Matt ahead of them. I slip back and walk behind Cooper and Jim.

I'm astounded that he's done that. Why isn't he talking to his wife, or his mate? I stretch my neck, rolling my head from side to side to stretch out the muscles. It's no big deal. I can talk to Cooper tonight and tomorrow.

The Mount Gower climb has been overshadowed by football and fame. Yet the conversation isn't about asking Coop his opinion, it's all about telling and wanting confirmation, or recognition, or acknowledgement.

I've never experienced this. No one is this interested in triathlons.

And then it hits me. They are. It's to a lesser degree but there are fanatics everywhere. Often it's a retired triathlete, or a failed one, or someone injured, who captures you and dissects each leg, each race, each competitor. It happens. It's happened to me. You're stuck, caught in a web where you can't upset them because they're a fan, so you can't get away.

'Excuse me. Excuse me.' I push past each pair to catch up to Greg. 'Greg, I'm really sorry to do this but it's getting late and Cooper and I need to run along to catch a night dive. It's been a fantastic trip, thank you, but do you mind if we take off?'

'Not at all. Sorry, I didn't realise you had to get back.'

'It's no trouble. We can run and make up time. Thanks Margaret, Sue, Jim and Matt. It's been a great day.'

Cooper is looking at me as if I've sprouted a pair of horns from my head. Or maybe it's my nose growing from the lies I've told. But he doesn't disagree. He makes his farewells and we jog away from the group. When we reach flatter ground we stride out and stretch into a run. The tension in my body eases.

'Sorry I lied.' I flick a glance towards Cooper who is laughing silently. His face is again relaxed and the old Cooper is there.

'I'm not.' He flashes that knee-weakening grin at me and I try not to lose stride but it's difficult.

We run home along the flat ground at a fast pace and it's a strain to keep up with him but the exhilaration is something else. I feel young, alive, vibrant, buzzing. I'm tired but wired. The stress of the day's discoveries lessens. Air blows over my face, tangy with sea salt, cool and refreshing.

By the time we're home, we fall through the door, both panting. I bend over to catch my breath. 'God, Coop, I didn't think you'd ever break a sweat.'

He grins, that knee-weakener on serious mega-wattage. 'Samantha Caine, why did you lie to those nice people?'

I catch his intense gaze, meet his deep chocolate stare. I should be flippant. I should say I needed his body. But this moment demands the truth. Although my stomach turns knots thinking about admitting why I lied, a tiny part of my heart is ajar, waiting to see where this leads.

'I couldn't listen to them any more. Geez, Coop. You weren't a person to them, you were a topic, a commodity. I couldn't stand watching you close up. I couldn't bear it any more.' My voice tapers off because he has a look that I can't read and my stomach has flipped over itself and is strangling my guts. I can't breathe and I'm scared I'm going to puke.

'You lied for me, to protect me?' His voice gives me no inkling as to what he's thinking either.

'Fuck. It was only a white lie, a tiny one. I didn't think you'd mind. I'm sorr—'

'Don't you dare apologise.' Cooper steps towards me and captures my hand in one of his, the other cups my cheek and lifts my face upwards. His thumb strokes across my cheek. Strong and soothing. 'Sam, what am I going to do without you?' His lips catch mine and his kiss disturbs my insides. My heart has been pushed wide open and I'm not sure I want to jam it closed again.

There's this part of me that hurts, though. And I need to face that part before I can have any portion of my heart available.

I pull away from the kiss. One step backwards gives me the distance to think. I draw in a deep breath. 'You played for Australia. Why didn't you tell me that?'

He shrugs.

'I raved on about the Olympics and you didn't think to say you'd represented Australia too?' My heart's thumping and I'm more wired up than I should be. It's like everything is escalating.

'You didn't rave, Sam, I enjoyed listening and hearing about your experiences.'

My teeth gnaw my lower lip. He's avoiding answering. I need to nail this. I need to work through these things that have stirred up enough to bug me. 'I'm glad you enjoyed it but wouldn't it have been better if we shared? Compare, contrast, discuss the same experience.' I wave my hand as I try to get across my thoughts.

It's trite when I say the words aloud. How do I explain that I feel cheated because he knows all my experiences and I don't know his?

'I ... Yes, I suppose I should have said something, but...' He threads his fingers through his hair and his gaze avoids mine. He shifts a little further away, turns his head slightly, and folds his arms across his chest. 'I didn't know you well enough to tell you then. But you're right. I should have told you. It's just ... I don't know how to explain it.'

'Try.'

'Did you see Jim today?' I nod. 'Most people are like him. And if they aren't, then...' He shrugs. 'It sounds like I'm skiting.'

'Oh, and I didn't sound like that?'

He holds up a finger and thumb a few centimetres apart before giving me his trademark grin. 'Only a tiny bit.'

I swat his bicep, my anger dissipating quickly. One stupid grin and I weaken. How bad am I? 'Are you saying I was skiting?'

He chuckles. 'Only enough to lure me into wanting you.'

Laughing, I swat his arm harder. 'I did not lure you.'

'You did so. Everything you do is alluring.'

'Oh, like the wolf-whistle you hated.'

He leans right over me, his chest brushing against my nipples, his breath skimming across my neck. 'No one's ever wolf-whistled me before.'

'Are you kidding?' I'm laughing and I can't tell if he's serious or joking.

'I never kid.' His lips nibble at my neck, along my collarbone up to my shoulder, then along my ear and jaw. I lean into him. Concentrating on the wet heat he's trailing across me. The cool air of the room drifts across the damp trails, making me quiver. He reads this as arousal, and I am in no position to argue. All my worry vanishes in my haze of lust.

We're still hot and sweaty from the day and the run home but the sweat only increases my arousal. His scent is strong, filling my mind with only him. My body slips against his. My arms slide freely around his neck. I drag my hands down his damp T-shirt and then struggle to pull it over his head without losing contact with him.

It's impossible to undress and kiss. We break apart and clothes fly. Then we're together again, slithering against one another, tasting and touching. He presses me against the wall and I climb his body trying to be in a position to take him inside me. It's hot and completely heady. His cock presses hard between my thighs and I rock over the head waiting for his surging entry thrust but he holds off. A second too long.

'Coop?' All my frustration comes out in his name.

He just grins and holds me still.

'Forgetting something?'

I stare at him. Nothing comes to mind except the pounding need for him. I squirm again. And stop.

'Oh my God.' A chill slides down my spine. 'Oh, thank God you stopped.'

Cooper puts an arm under my butt and holds me clinging on to his hips. 'Stay there. I can grab one. Just don't squirm.'

I can't believe I didn't remember safety. I've never done that. Or not in the last 20 years, anyhow. I tip my head back as self-recrimination hits.

'Don't you dare leave me.' Cooper's words are punctuated with a tongue licking across my nipple, first one then the other. 'That's better.' He moves and I lean to help, pulling out the condom and holding it for him. He sheathes himself.

'I can't bel—'

His mouth on mine cuts off any more words. Again I'm pressed to the wall and his cock presses for entry. But my mind, with all its worries and doubts, has kicked in and Cooper seems to know it. He takes my nipple in his mouth and sucks, biting, flicking, extending the tender flesh between tight lips. His hands hold my hips tightly, thumbs digging in hard, directing my hips in a slow rolling movement while his mouth feasts on the other nipple. My brain turns to lust and his cock surges inside me. I arch, cry out, then drop against his hips trying for deeper or harder or more. Something.

It's fast and hard but slower than this morning's efforts. And somehow, even in all the fury and haste, there's emotion I haven't felt before. A togetherness, the sort I've never experienced and so can't identify. Maybe it's just that we peak simultaneously, with no effort at all. That we fly at the exact second without waiting or coaxing. The synchronicity amplifying my orgasm so that it's harder, stronger, deeper and more shattering. And leaves me lying limply over his shoulder.

I'm lucky that Cooper doesn't weaken. He strides to the shower with me still attached. The spray hits me hard and I leap. His cock comes free and he discards the condom before gently lowering me to the floor. Then he washes me with a tenderness that almost breaks me. He shampoos my hair, and holds me close while he washes himself. Then he bundles me against his huge chest, holding me close and pressing butterfly kisses across my face. He dries me and wraps me in a towel, sitting me on the ledge to wait while he dries himself.

Once we're both dry and clad in towels, he lifts me to his chest again and carries me to the bed. He sits on the edge but doesn't release me. His hand skims my hair. His lips press against my temple.

I know I should move or speak or make some action, but nothing feels right. Nothing except sitting here wrapped in Cooper. My hand rests against his chest. Not moving, just being. I'm content. I don't want to be anywhere else but here. I don't want to be with anyone else but him. The little opening in my heart now gapes wide, like magpies singing at dawn.

Chapter 14

For my last full day, Cooper's hired a double sea kayak for us to paddle out around the island, or in the lagoon if it's too rough outside.

My smile must be a mile wide. 'I can't believe you thought of this. It's perfect.'

'There's one thing though.' I turn in query and he grins. 'I get to be at the back.'

I laugh and wave him towards the rear. 'Control freak.' It doesn't bother me where I sit, though sitting behind Cooper watching his muscles flex would have been a treat.

We don life vests, take waterproof bags of lunch and necessities, and slip into the kayak. We've both paddled before but it'll be interesting to see how we manage together.

Once we get going, I don't know why I even thought there'd be a problem; we paddle together like we've been doing it for years. Cooper must be matching my strokes because there's no clash of paddles, just smooth gliding across the water.

'Are we heading out round the island?' I ask once we've settled into a rhythm and are heading towards the edge of the lagoon.

'I'd like to. It's calm and the forecast is good. It should be like this all day.'

'Awesome, let's go.'

From the lagoon, we paddle to the south-west towards the mountains. The water is crystal clear. We stop paddling to gaze at the bottom of the water, watch fish and the occasional small reef shark or turtle. We drift along in the current for a while. It's peaceful.

In the shadow of Mount Lidgbird is Little Island, a large, rugged rock covered in stunted plants and sea birds. It's nature at its rawest and harshest. Hard rock to grow on and heavy salty air to live in. 'This place amazes me.' My voice is all breathy and whispering.

We start paddling again when the ocean current swirls us in a new direction.

'So, Coop, what does it feel like to represent your country?'

While we paddle, he fills me in on all I missed in our previous conversation. It's a balm to my soul to hear more about his personal life.

The slopes below Mount Gower are forests of palms and banyans. Bright green against the black basalt rock. It's beautiful. Not going anywhere. Solid. Safe. Kind of like Cooper.

We're talking about our achievements and wins when Cooper says, 'I value my club wins, my state wins, but when you win for your country in a tough, close international game, I think that's the greatest achievement you can ever have.'

I can only agree. 'Nothing compares to standing there with your country's honour resting on your shoulders.'

'Is it a heavy burden when you're competing on your own?'

'Never. It's a privilege. Something you've worked towards. Something you've earned. The thrill is immense.'

'It's the same for me. Being selected as an Australian team member is such an achievement and running on in that jersey, I can't put words to how it feels.'

We keep paddling and chatting. The rhythmic strokes come naturally to me. I stare at the beauty of the mountains towering straight up from the sea. The sunshine sparkles across the tiny wavelets, like shimmering diamonds. The sun warms me, as does our conversation. I'm relaxed and happier than I have been in a long time. Sharing our experiences is more than heart-warming, my whole being is filled.

I know a lot more about Cooper the football player. A side that he's not shown before. I've seen his competitive nature, but not learned his love of the game, the hard work he puts in to be at his peak, the sacrifices, injuries, concerns, and camaraderie shared.

It isn't a one-sided conversation at all. He asks as much about me as I do him. It's refreshing to find someone who shares a conversation and listens as well as talks.

When the conversation naturally wanes, we paddle in silence for a good distance. The peaks no longer loom over us as we round the southern tip. A rocky island appears on the right covered in white splotches and sea birds.

We paddle around the southern tip and along the eastern side. A large scree-covered slope dominates the edge of the island. Palms and dense vegetation make a thick green blanket over the foot of the black mountains.

We talk of family, friends, life. Random topics that come to mind. Tidbits of information. It's easy and fun and light, but dear Lord, I want him. I'm learning about his mind and I love that but I still want his body. Again.

We glide past a peninsula, thin and angular jutting from the island. As we round it, large red rocky outcrops dot the northern side.

'Do you reckon there are any secluded beaches along here?'

Cooper laughs. 'Is the paddling too much action for you, Sam?'

I chuckle. Hopefully sexily. I don't want to admit my lust out loud.

We paddle past another tight point. A few islands are off to our right, and I wonder if the islands have beaches. They look too rocky and craggy. I glance ashore and spy a strip of sand.

'There's a beach.' I exclaim it as if it's momentous. 'Will we go have a look?'

Cooper chuckles. 'Just a look?' I guess my over-enthusiasm tips him off that I'm after more than a look at the sand.

I turn and flash him a grin. 'Yeah, just a look.' Sarcasm drips off each word.

We head towards the strip of sand, pale against the lush vegetation. When we're close to the beach, the bottom of the kayak scrapes over submerged rocks. At first it doesn't matter, we can see the darkness of them in the water and paddle around them, but soon the entire water seems filled by submerged rocks and I can't determine their depths.

'If we got out, we could probably float the kayak in over the rocks.' It's the only way I can see us getting to the beach intact.

'And how do we get out without capsizing?' He has a good point. It doesn't take much to tip these.

'If we each got our legs out and sat astride, then faced out and slid off at the same time we'd be right, wouldn't we?'

'Except I weigh about twice what you do.'

I chuckle. 'I'll think heavy.'

'You really want to go to the beach?'

I turn my head, and my eyes stretch wide open. I flick my tongue across dry lips. It's the secluded beach we've been looking for the whole time and he's questioning going in. Have I lost my touch?

He laughs. 'Forget I said that. Get your legs out.'

We wriggle, rocking the kayak vigorously, until finally my feet are dangling in the water each side of the kayak.

'Left or right?' he asks.

'I'll go left. That okay?'

'On three we'll swing to our side. You think heavy. We'll hold there and check the water before sliding in.'

With much laughter, a lot of kayak rocking and water splashing, we're in the water and heading to the beach, dodging rocks and tugging paddles and the kayak between us. We drag the gear up the beach so the rising tide won't leave us stranded.

'Do you reckon we're the only people here?' I scan the beach, the ocean, and the rainforest behind us. There appears to be no one anywhere around. No tracks lead onto the beach through the forest, well, none I can see. Unless a boat comes along, or a plane, we should be alone.

'Looks like it's just us. So what's your plan?' Cooper asks.

'Plan? I have no plan.' I do, but I'm not admitting it. My plan isn't fancy; I want sex.

'And if I have a plan?' His shiny eyes seem to dance as his grin slips from knee-weakening to completely carnal.

My stomach lurches. Boy, am I glad we detoured to the beach. 'If you have a plan, then I'm all for it.' I grin, hoping to keep my tone light instead of revealing the lustful longing that's coursing through me. *Hell. What kind of plan is it?*

Cooper flicks his chin up and his head gives a bit of a nod. I wonder if he's trying to invent a plan or if he already had some idea. Maybe he's worried about how I'll take it. My lungs freeze mid-breath. Last time he wanted clean-skin sex and I freaked. *Oh God, please don't let me freak this time.*

I suck in a breath and his eyes dilate as he stares at the small frills on the edge of my bikini top. The tiny hairs on my arm quiver as if a breeze has blown across them. My spine tingles. My stomach clenches and deeper inside, my womb does a kind of barrel-roll and juices seep into my cunt. *Fuck, he could make me come with his gaze.*

'Cooper.' My voice is strained and his name comes out in at least three disjointed syllables. 'What's the plan?'

He takes a breath and I can't tear my stare away from his stomach muscles bunching and releasing. The way his chest lifts and falls, and his tight nipples. It feels like he's breathed the breath out of me.

'I want to watch you.' Said so simply, his deeper, aroused voice slips across the wettest part of me as if it's his finger sliding along the slick folds. I shudder from my toes to my scalp. I don't need any more direction. If he wants to watch, I can give him a show.

I reach behind for the string on my bikini top but before I can untie the bow, he stops me.

'Not like that. I want a triathlon.'

My hands drop to my hips and I stare at him. 'You want me to swim, bike and run?' The unspoken words are 'instead of sex?' but I don't need to utter them as my tone surely implies it.

'Yes. I'm going to lie in the shallows where there are no rocks and I want you to swim around me. Then I want to watch you cycle where the tide laps, and run down the beach so when I catch you, you're wet and hot.' His words shouldn't be sexy. His idea shouldn't be arousing. But I'm breathy, wet and wanting.

'How do I do that?' My mind is jumbled up with words and images and need. I can't separate them to make sense of his plan. I can't for the life of me think through each phase and transition. How do I swim and transition to cycle, cycle then transition to running? I can only think of the finish, and that's not the way to get through a triathlon.

'You'll work it out, Sam.' He flashes a quick grin as he skims his shorts off.

Oh, yeah, great way for me to work it out. I'm already in a lust-daze, and seeing him naked and aroused is so going to help.

While I'm staring, he walks into the sea. The waves lick at his calves, then the backs of his knees, his thighs. And then his butt sinks into the water and he lies amongst the waves. He ducks his head back so he's submerged and then sprays water through his lips like a fountain. My breath catches. He could be a god of the sea, except I'm pretty sure they're not as buff as him.

Swimming around his glorious body is going to be fun. And I haven't been banned from touching, or tasting, or any other pleasure-taking. This could end up being my favourite type of triathlon.

Ditching my swimmers, I wade into the water and make a shallow dive so I glide out and under him. I pop up on his far side, take a breath and then duck under. The water is so clear, I can open my eyes and make out his shape; not the specific details because it's blurry but enough to enjoy myself. I brush the pad of my thumb along the veins of his arm, dipping into the bend of his elbow and up along his bicep swell. My hand moulds around his shoulder joint and I align my body beneath his, peeking my head up next to his to take another breath.

Breath taken and lungs filled with air, I scull with one hand until I'm slipping underneath his body, one hand trailing over his skin from shoulder, over shoulder blade, down to waist, the top of his butt and over the swell of his buttock, down his thigh, behind his knee, over the rounded calf before cupping his foot and lifting my head up for another breath.

This time after submerging, I swim under his legs to his buttocks and roll beneath him so I can blow a stream of bubbles along his spine from base to neck. I hope they tickle. I hope they dance along his flesh like spidery touches. I hope it's worth the head spin I get when I pop up near his shoulder, gasping for another breath.

'Try not to drown doing this, Sam.' His dry comment makes me smile. The head of his cock, poking further out of the water than any other part of his body, has me grinning.

I lie beneath him, held up by the buoyant water, head next to his, knees loosely hooked on his thighs to keep my body against him. Turning my head, I nibble against his neck, beneath his ear, suck on his earlobe, bite along his ear and then back again. My tongue slips along his jaw before sliding down his neck to his collarbone. I'm enjoying myself way too much when Cooper's arms start to wave underwater. I stand and steady him before I drown us both.

'Sorry, got carried away. I promise I won't drown you.' Laughing, I move between his legs and hook them around my hips. I can't drown him but the way I'm feeling, I hope I'll notice if I am.

My hands close over the top of his tight thighs. My fingers massage the tense muscles, slipping ever upwards until I curl them around the base of his cock. I lean forward to taste the head and before my mouth touches his flesh, I see his arms waving in the water, sculling.

'You could tell me before you sink, Coop.'

'It's okay. I didn't want you to stop.'

I chuckle and slip one hand beneath his butt to keep him afloat before stroking his cock with my right hand.

'I thought you were going to taste,' he says in a kind of strangled voice, although maybe he's just swallowed too much salt water.

I grin. 'I got distracted.' But I don't taste. My fist dips up and down, water swirling with each movement. Waves wash rhythmically and I time my hand to the ocean. The water adds to the slickness and cools his heated flesh but the muscle beneath the skin is hard and unaffected by the cool ocean.

When my head doesn't dip to his cock, Cooper relaxes, no longer waiting or expectant. He stretches his arms out wide and floats. His gaze flicks between my face and the bright blue sky. His hips rock in time with my hands and the waves. He seems to lose himself in the rocking motion.

Only then do I bend and close my mouth around the tip of his cock. He doesn't move, only a flinch lets me know he feels the heated moist cavern of my mouth. Then I lick the flat of my tongue across the top of his cock. One strong lapping motion. A hiss escapes his lips.

I make him wait for more.

My fist still pumps and my mouth surrounds the head but my tongue is kept tucked away.

I wait an agonising 10 waves before I curl my tongue around his cock, flicking and tasting, sampling and sliding. I love this part. I love the feel of his cock against my tastebuds.

A larger-than-normal wave washes over us and I leap up spluttering. Water has washed into my mouth and nose, robbing me of breath and burning me with salty tang.

Instead of complaining, Cooper laughs. We're standing waist deep, laughing, and I'm spluttering. Not the best path to arousal.

'God, that wasn't meant to happen.' I heave the words between coughing.

'You mean you've never been dumped by a rogue wave in the swim leg?'

I look at him with something like a quizzical frown, I hope. 'I know you're good, but there's no way you planned that. No way in the world.'

He laughs and slings his arm across my shoulder. 'I am good, you're right, but not that good.' He grins and plonks a kiss on the tip of my nose. 'I think the cycle leg is next.'

'With a lousy transition,' I mutter as I drag myself out of my splutter. In triathlons, transitions can make or break a race, and my change from swim to cycle here is terrible. Thank goodness it's not a race. 'How does the cycle go?'

'I was imagining you in the wet sand, legs in the air, cycling.'

I stop and stare. Splutter completely gone. 'You ... what?'

He grins and winks before waving his hand towards the sand. 'Beautiful secluded beach. Nice lazy way to cycle. Awesome view for me.'

I shake my head in a no-way-am-I-doing-that way.

'What's the problem, Sam? There's nothing I haven't seen. Aren't you up for some aerial bike riding?'

He's right. He has seen all I've got. So why am I balking at exposing myself? Why am I worried about this?

I've got no answers.

No answers at all.

No matter how hard I try to find an answer, nothing's coming.

I shrug. 'I was just trying to anticipate what awful transition you have in store for me next time.' I grin and wander out of the water to the wet sand, hoping I can get high enough not to get a crotch full of sandy water from a big wave, but low enough not to have dry sand up my crack. It's a delicate decision.

When I find a position I hope is perfect, I plonk myself down, slide my hands beside my hips, then lift my hips up onto my hands and I'm in a shoulder stand. 'Is this the pose you're after?'

Cooper stands to the side, a smirk on his lips but cock still hard. 'Perfect.'

If his cock goes flaccid, this bike leg will be short.

I move my legs as if riding a bike, and try not to erupt into giggles. This is surely not romantic or arousing or even attractive.

'How long do I have to do this for?' I ask as my legs hurl around in circles. I'm not looking at him because I feel like a fool and I can't bear to see him laughing at me.

A cool breeze whips across my heated cunt and little shudders tremble through me. I let out a tiny moan I hope he doesn't hear. I dart my gaze to the side to look. The sight makes my head whip around so I can see better.

His hand is fisted tightly around a purple-headed cock, and he's pumping hard. His face is contorted like he's aroused and holding back. And when he catches my gaze, his eyes are dark pools I could drown in. Suddenly cycling isn't so crazy.

I spread my thighs and pedal harder. The breeze teases, a wave scoots too far up the beach and brushes against my buttocks. I jump but keep pedalling. The water isn't too bad.

Every so often a wave brushes against me, teasing gently and I'm almost waiting to feel them. To have the wetness slide against my butt crack. The coolness of the breeze and the air above the water washes over my heated core. The damp of the sand softens beneath my hips. I seep further into a state like euphoria, as if I am doing a race. Nothing will drag me out of the zone.

Until a deep guttural sound comes from Cooper.

'No,' I say. 'No coming yet.'

'Then run.' The intensity of those two words has me roll over and scramble to my feet. I take two steps and feel the blood pounding but my head's light. I shake my head to get the blood flowing upwards and run. The air pushes against me, cooling, tantalising, skimming. My feet beat against the wet sand, splashing as the larger waves hit the beach. There's such freedom in running naked.

I hear Cooper behind me. Loud splashes as he races to catch me. But I'm light as a bird and flying down the beach. I step up the pace so I'm running as hard as I can.

But why am I running from him? Why make such an effort when I ultimately want him to catch me? Only my deeply competitive spirit keeps me racing. I do want him to catch me, but damn it, he can work hard first and earn me.

When I'm out of beach, I slow. I thought of running onto the dry sand but dry sand and sex doesn't do it for me. So I stay where the sand's wet, slowing so he can catch me and wrap me against his hard pounding muscles.

And that's just what he does. He opens his arms and swoops down on me, wrapping me against his chest, my legs between his, and his lips claim mine. The kiss holds nothing back. Both of us are panting hard, so the kiss is deep but broken into pieces to allow breathing.

A bits-and-pieces kiss shouldn't have the ability to sear your soul but this one burns mine. As our tongues duel and our lips meld, my innards churn—tensing, releasing, tumbling. I'm a mess of emotional madness. It's exhilarating and terrifying.

Our bodies rub against each other. Hands touching, grabbing, holding, sliding. I can't get enough of him and it seems it's mutual.

I open my legs so his cock can probe, seeking my core. But that's not enough. I lift a leg to wrap around his hip and draw him closer but instead he eases me onto the wet sand and follows me.

Cooper straddles me, holding himself up on his hands and knees, and the kiss deepens. No more breaks, gasps or pauses. This is a full-blown moment of kissing. The deep pashing of two bodies in sync.

My hands roam his chest, arms, shoulders and neck. I can't keep still. Sensation floods me. His silken skin. Rough stubble. Solid muscle. Fine dusting of chest hair. Cording of veins. Swell of pecs. Tight beads of nipples. The decadent taste of his tongue. The pressure of his lips. The moist heat of his mouth. I writhe, lifting my hips to nudge at his cock. I rub and push my hips to his. I need him joined to me, filling me.

He pulls away as I'm wrapping my legs around his hips to attempt to pull him into me.

'We can't, Sam.'

I grip his shoulders and try to pull him back into the kiss, ignoring the words.

'Sam, the fucking condoms are in the kayak.'

His words penetrate my haze and I stop fighting.

For a few long seconds we just stare at each other, like we're both catching our breath, or sorting our mind.

He recovers first. 'I'll race you back there.'

I shake my head. If we race back it won't be like this. I won't feel like this.

I know I should get up and swim to cool off. I know I should do something sensible, instead I reach up and kiss him, slowly, lingering a lot.

'Do you think we have a chance at long term?' I ask, my lips brushing his as I speak.

'I'll do anything I can to fit you into my life. But I thought you only wanted a fling?'

I glance away from him, scrunch my eyes tight and bite my lips together. I didn't realise he knew. I look back at him, right into his eyes. Time slows.

'I've changed. Is that okay?'

'You mean you want more than a holiday fling?' His question is quietly spoken as if he's holding his breath.

Chapter 15

I nod slowly, not breaking eye contact. My breath is caught in the emotional cauldron inside me. I know I should breathe but everything seems to be waiting for his answer, even my lungs.

'I can work with that.' He gives his usual grin, which for once does nothing to my knees. Instead it puts a delirious grin to my face, and makes me hook my legs around his hips, my arms around his neck and the kiss I begin is, incredibly, more heated than before. I could combust.

It takes only a few moments for me to be writhing beneath him, eagerly seeking his cock. But then I realise I haven't quite spelled it all out to him, and knowing him, he won't take advantage of my passion to do what he thinks I may not want.

I pull my mouth from the kiss. 'If we're talking some kind of exclusive relationship, where we work out the details later, can we skip protection?'

I watch as his expression vanishes, his face jerks back slightly and his eyes widen. 'Are you sure?'

'Positive.'

'You won't regret this in the aftermath?'

I shake my head. 'No. Not now.'

He smirks, so I know he's going to say something cheeky, but I probably deserve it.

'Is it because I play for Australia?'

When I arch my brow at him and scrunch my forehead, he explains. 'You know, I wasn't good enough unless I'd worn the green and gold.'

I laugh because his smirking grin tells me he's not serious. I know he doesn't believe that. I know he's lightening an intense moment and giving me time to change my mind in case I've made a hasty decision in a lust-fuelled state. It only makes me like him even more. And *like* is becoming too ridiculously weak a word for these feelings. It's love. But I can't admit that out loud.

'Yep, I'm like that. Only the best will do for me.' I press a gentle kiss against the edge of his lips. 'And you Cooper, are the best.' Our lips lock. Talking is over for now. From here on, it's all passion, clean-skin sex, and sensation. I haven't had skin sex since I was a gawky, fumbling teenager.

With Cooper there's no gawkiness, no fumbling. We move together with ease even in our desperation. He sits on his heels before he lifts my legs up and wiggles my hips up onto his thighs. 'I don't want you ripped to shreds by sand.' His hands lift my shoulders so I'm sitting on his lap.

How can I help but smile? What man thinks of sand abrading your back while he fucks you?

He holds me on his lap and our lips meet in a kiss that's both gentle and rough. Holding all the need, but somehow keeping it controlled. And that's the power of us, the expertise of him. He's strong and powerful but somehow restrained.

He breaks the kiss and laps against my lips with the tip of his tongue, tasting me like a rich dessert. I curl my hand around his cock. Hand closed tightly, I direct his cock along my slick folds. Starting with a silken brush over my throbbing clit, sliding between my wet lips, and finishing with a probe of my tight hole. Just the silken head pushing against my tightness. I want to tease first, please later.

The warmth of his cock is what I notice first. No gasp from cool latex or lube. Only the silken touch of skin as warm as my own, sliding through moisture. I wonder if he perceives the difference. Does he enjoy the silken-wet warmth of my cunt instead of the tight confinement of latex?

Looking up into his face makes my blood heat and fizz. His eyes are closed, head tipped back, lips parted and jaw clenched tight. His teeth are just visible and I'm tempted to push my tongue between his lips and slide it against his pearly whites. A hiss escapes him as I press myself onto his cock probing my core. I didn't mean to take his cock-head inside but now it is, I can't hold back. Clinging to his shoulders, I lower myself onto him, ensuring I take him slowly so I feel every centimetre of solid silken warmth.

Both our heads are thrown back as I settle on the full, glorious length of him. The sunlight warms my face and shoulders. Dancing spots dart across my closed eyelids. My whole body is warmed from the outside and in.

'God, you're wet.' His voice is strained but also holds something like awe or wonder or shock. Maybe it does feel incredible for him too. I stare at him for a few seconds, my pupils adjusting to the blazing sun, before we both move and our lips meet in a kiss that's as wet and needy as I am.

His hands tighten on my hips, directing my movements through pressure and the slightest forward motion. I don't need a lot of encouragement. The swollen heat of him inside me demands action.

I rise and fall, slowly at first, but the tension is too much and as our kisses turn fast, tongues duelling and teeth clashing, my thighs pump me up and down his length, faster and faster.

My breasts jiggle in the warm air, creating a little cool draught. My nipples have tightened, silently begging for his touch but his hands still grasp my hips.

I arch so my nipples rub against the solid spheres of his pecs, and we thrust together. Then he pulls from the kiss, his mouth open in a soundless word. His head tips back just enough so his chest pushes harder against my throbbing breasts.

His fingers almost mash my hip bones, his grip becomes uncomfortable, but before I can do anything about it, his cock thrusts upwards once, twice, three, four times, before his body tenses and a growl erupts from deep inside him. I'm flooded. Flooded by heat, warmth and moisture. His cock thrusts freely and deeply.

My clit is crushed each time he strains into me. Exquisite heat fills me. A throbbing deep inside sets up and then I burst, as if every cell within me has swollen and popped. I'm drowning, flooded by sensation. Sitting in a pool of hot sticky seed and molten lust. My hands grasp his biceps, holding on for life, while I'm speared by his cock, over and over. Wave after wave of sensation hits me.

It's a release like none I've ever had. My whole self has been torn asunder and mended. However, I must have acquired new bits or am missing bits or have not been put together right because I feel wrong. Not like me at all. The world looks different. The sunlight is more intense. The sky a brighter blue. The sand brilliant white. I can hear the sweep of wings when a tern flies past. Cooper's heart thumps beside me. I can almost hear the whoosh of blood as it pumps through arteries. My body is lighter, either defying gravity or I've lost a lot of kilos through good sex.

I'm still joined to Cooper, resting on his knees, my arms holding his, my head against his shoulder, his arms around me holding me close. Tears drip down my cheeks. I don't think I can ever move again. I don't think I'm capable of rising free of his cock. And I don't think I can ever let him go.

Yet tomorrow I go home.

The thought is like an icicle to my heart, stabbing and chilling in one action.

This isn't me.

I don't get emotional after sex. I don't get attached to partners. I don't lose my focus. But right now I've no idea what to do with my life. No idea what to focus on.

'Jesus, Sam.' I hear the words but the voice doesn't sound like Cooper's. 'Are you okay?' His hand scoots along my spine, calming and soothing. His touch soaks in, easing me.

'I don't know.' My voice doesn't sound like mine either. 'Are you?'

We're still connected, wrapped around each other, when a large wave dances against my feet. Cooper jerks, sharply pulling us apart. My head clears a little.

Cooper curses. 'Bloody wave.' It must have run right underneath him. I'm lucky he didn't drop me off his lap.

I kiss his neck, working my way around to his face. He brushes my cheekbones with his thumbs before our lips meet in a gentle kiss. A soft joining. Our lips move over each other, tongues just touch and retreat. My fingers spear through his hair, holding his head lightly, the short threads tickle. His fingers massage my scalp, holding me gently in place.

I've never felt this in tune with anyone. Never been so caught up in the web of another. As much as the thought scares me, I also have hope. Not only hope, but joy. A feeling like finishing a race, running up that last stretch, alone with the pain and hurt, but also with hope and joy at the thought you've earned it. Earned the success. Earned the personal best time. Or even earned the win.

The kiss ends and we sit together. Silent. Still, except for ragged breaths.

'I'm falling in love with you.' The words that pour from my mouth stun me. I stare at Cooper. My gaze locked to his. My breaths timed to his. My words hanging heavy in the cool air.

'I know, Sam. I feel the same.'

'I don't know what to do about it. I don't know if I can—'

His thumb brushes my lips, halting my words.

'We'll work it out together. Our way.'

I nod. It's all I'm capable of.

It takes a long time before we move, each unfolding from our cramped position slowly before stretching tight muscles.

'Need a swim?' I ask as the knots loosen.

'Sounds good.' He captures my hand and together we take a dip. A quiet swim basking in our togetherness. Touching like we're discovering each other for the first time. Kissing softly, reverently. Brushing bodies briefly. A gentle, quiet time like we haven't shared before.

After the swim, we head back to the kayak, have a quick bite to eat and then continue on the journey.

Once we're paddling, Cooper says, 'Let's see if we can work a few things out before we get back, okay?'

Genuinely confused, I ask, 'What things?'

'I don't do relationships, Sam, and neither do you.' My heart clenches. The ocean slips past, my arms keep moving, hips rocking in time between strokes but I've no idea where they're getting the oxygen and blood supply from. My heart and lungs have shut down.

He continues. 'But rules can be broken, especially for someone like you.'

A whoosh of air escapes my lips and I can't mask it with the dip of the paddle or the surge of the sea. He has to know it's me and relief, hand in hand.

The silence lasts for so long—I figure he's waiting for me to speak. He hasn't asked a question so I'm not sure what I'm meant to say. I go with the relationship thing because I can't think of anything else. 'I don't have rules. I just suck at relationships. I am willing to try though.'

'Why do you suck at relationships?'

Good question and I wish I knew the answer. I shrug. 'I don't know what to say most of the time. I don't know how people take me. I don't understand the game playing. I don't have time, or at least I didn't, to stuff around working things out.' I dip the paddle in for another stroke while I think about what I said. I've left out the important bit. 'I don't get that with you. Oh, well, some of it. I never know what to say.'

'With me?'

I nod.

'When?'

'Even now. I don't know if this is what you want me to say, if this is what you want to talk about. I don't know where we're going.'

Cooper barks in a kind of laugh and a scoff. 'I don't have an agenda. I just want to know what you're thinking. I didn't know you found it hard. I thought you were straight, honest, telling me what you thought?'

'I am. With you, that's what I do. That's why you're different.'

'Okay, so that's a good thing, right? It means we're ready to give a relationship a try?'

I shuffle in my seat, miss a couple of strokes and then give up trying to paddle. I rest the oar across my lap. 'I'd love that, except I don't know that I can handle the fame, the publicity thing you have. I flounder and you take it in your stride. I imagine it's even worse in Melbourne and I don't know if I can manage that.'

Cooper makes a few strokes to correct our course and the quiet dip and swoosh of the oar calms me. His paddle stops and the kayak wobbles as he shifts. His fingers grasp my right shoulder. A squeeze and a brush across my skin centres me. It's like I've said the right thing again, even when it scares me.

'It is more than what we've seen here. It's not much worse than Jim on the walk though. It's not like the paparazzi stalk me.'

I turn around and flash him a grin before picking up the paddle again. We make our way along the island in silent contemplation. As we pass Neds Beach, we wave to the people.

'You'd be able to handle it, like you have here. And it gets easier the more it happens. Most people are a repeat of the person before, so you have lots of practice at the same questions, same answers. It's just patience, making a choice about how much to say, and dealing with people. I know you'll cope.'

'What if I run?' I know I do that too easily and I don't want to embarrass him.

'So long as you make up an excuse that has me running with you, I'm in.' Cooper laughs and I know he's making light of the truth. If I protect him, he'll look after me. He's honourable like that.

The Admiralty Islands are off to the right as we turn the corner and the northern part of the island with its rugged cliffs drifts past.

'Does our age difference bother you? I'll be pushing to fit kids in before it's too late, yet you're in no rush.'

He chuckles. 'It would bother me if I was 15, but I don't think about it.'

'Other people might.'

'I don't care what other people think. It's my life, my choice and my business.'

'What would you have done ... what were you planning for your life before we met?'

The northern cliffs go by and still there's no response. I wonder if I should rephrase the question, or if I've intruded, or if it's too difficult. I can't see his expression when I twist around because of the sunglasses, cap, and the shadow from its brim.

'Sorry. I shouldn't have pried.'

'It's not that. Ask me anything you want. I'm yours, Sam.' He rests his paddle but I keep stroking, slow and measured. I hope the rhythmic dip and pull will calm him as it did me. Sometimes finding an answer is a struggle.

'I don't have a plan. I can't think beyond football. I know I should. I know I need to think out plan B in case of injury or something but I never have. Football's been everything. Other people have partners, relationships, kids, the happy family but I've never found anyone to fit in, not easily, and so it's just been footy. One hundred per cent. I don't have a clue what else to do. Football's my life. I haven't thought beyond it.' He takes a breath after all the words have run out almost on top of each other.

I feel his desperation. He told me he lived for football and I half expected this answer but the pain of him saying it is difficult to hear. I know what it's like to leave the sport you love. To leave the safety of training. I don't know if I should say anything yet or if he has more. So I paddle quietly. A few more moments of waiting won't hurt.

'How did you decide to retire, Sam?'

I'm glad I'm not looking at him when I have to answer this one. 'I trained with a kid who was desperate to move along her career. She was good. Really good. But I kept beating her. She was 20 and still being beaten by me but it was getting difficult. Niggling injuries bothered me. Recovery time was getting longer. I got selected and she missed out, again. She was gutted. I didn't feel good about beating her this time. She was on the rise, and I was on the decline. She deserved her chance before she lost the competitive edge.' I shake my head. 'I don't know why but I retired my spot, then retired from competition. It was a gut feeling that I don't truly understand. I wanted to go out on top. I didn't want to ruin a kid's career. I had the offer of coaching. Things seemed to fall into place.'

We paddle on in silence.

'Did you know what you wanted from life after?' He asks the question as we make our way past Mount Eliza and around the tip.

I laugh. 'You ask that after being with me this week and seeing how messed up I am about partners, kids?'

'I don't know what I want from life after football. I can't honestly imagine my life without it. And then I came here and met you, and you mentioned kids, and I can see a hazy image.'

My heart's in my throat and the butterflies in my stomach are more like stampeding buffalo. 'What's the image?'

'I can see us with a tribe of kids here, at the beach, racing along the sand, teaching them to snorkel, laughing together at their excitement, hiking up the hills, exploring.' He takes a deep breath. 'And it's not a bad picture.'

His image is well painted. I can see boys like him, girls like him, boys like me, girls like me, other kids joining in. It's a terrifying picture, but he's right, there's good about it too.

'I'm too old for a tribe of kids.' It's all I can get from my mouth. And I'm pleased I can say anything after mentally seeing his vision.

'If we started today, we could have three or four in a few years, couldn't we?' The laughter in his voice tells me he's jesting, but sometimes the truth is hidden in jest.

Started today? Three or four? My poor brain's panicking but all I manage to say is, 'I'm still covered by contraceptive. By the time it wears off, what if it's too late and we can't have any kids?' If Cooper only wants children, this will stop him.

The kayak wobbles as Cooper moves. 'If we can't have any, then we adopt or foster or borrow nieces and nephews. You're important to me, Sam. You.'

My heart almost thumps out of my chest. 'This is going awfully quickly. We've only known each other a week.' I can't physically run but oh, boy, I can do it mentally. We're coming past North Beach and almost back into the lagoon. I half hope the conversation will end when the trip does.

Cooper laughs and splashes water at me from the end of his paddle. 'Sam, Sam, Sam. I got this kayak so you had nowhere to run when we had this discussion. Don't skip out on me now.'

'You hired the kayak to talk about kids?'

'It freaked you out so much, I wanted to see why. I wanted to understand you. I didn't think we'd seriously be talking about ... No, that's a lie. I wanted to talk about us but I didn't hope we'd get this far.'

I'm not sure if he means this far in our discussion, this far in a relationship, or even this far around the island, and I'm just too chicken to ask him to clarify.

'I think we're doing well for a week. If we didn't get along, I wouldn't have survived a few days, much less a week.' He sounds pleased, whether it's with himself, or with me, or us, I'm not sure.

I have to agree with him. I feel the same. 'I don't tolerate anyone for too long either. You're an exception.'

'So, where does this leave us?' His neutral tone and open question lets me run if I want to.

I clench my back teeth. I'm being a grown up and facing this. I'm not running. 'In a serious relationship, talking about moving, multiple kids and the future. Scaring the shit out of me. At the same time, I'm excited, or thrilled or shocked or something.'

'Thank God, we're on the same page.'

Cooper's words make me laugh and he joins in. Somehow it's not as terrifying when you can laugh.

We paddle back to the lagoon beach, our mood lighter.

The whole day has been incredible. The scenery and serenity astounding. Tranquil ocean, a small boat, great company, hairy conversations and perfect weather make it a day I'll never forget.

We beach the kayak and drag it up the sand. While we're retrieving our belongings, Brian calls out. 'I knew you two couldn't keep out of the water completely.'

We laugh, wave and go up to chat for a while before more goodbyes. Cooper and I head off.

'Do you need to go to your place, Sam, to get packed or organised?'

I laugh. 'I've hardly unpacked. I'll need 10 minutes in the morning to grab my stuff, that's all.'

He grins. 'Then my place it is.'

'No food?'

'It's already organised.' His smile has a slightly sheepish tinge to it but I can't complain. I'd be grumbling if he didn't spend the night with me. And he'd be growling if he wasn't fed.

Chapter 16

Back in Cooper's room for the last night, he has chowder delivered. Piping hot bowls, just like being at the restaurant. His thoughtfulness makes the chowder sweeter, saltier, thicker, richer.

Afterwards, we shower quickly before he brushes his fingers across the top of my shoulder. 'You got a touch of sun, even with sunscreen.'

'Not surprising since we spent all day out there. But at least it's not sore or really burned.' I grab my bottle of jojoba oil.

'Here, let me.' Cooper holds his hand out for the bottle and I pass it over. 'This feels nice,' he says as he squirts the oil into his palm.

'It's supposed to be the closest oil to our skin's. It soaks in fast and does a great job moisturising.'

He slathers oil across my shoulders with slick palms. My toes curl. Shoulder muscles, sore from the paddling, ease at his touch. He walks me towards the bed. 'Lie down and I'll make it good.'

I need no other encouragement.

I lie down and he sprays more drops of oil against my back before his hands work to massage it in. Heavenly decadence. Feather soft pillow, dreamy mattress, man with huge gentle hands, oil, muscles relaxing. I couldn't be in a better place.

'We don't have plans after tonight, Sam, and I'd like some.' His hands remain gentle, his voice is quiet but there's steel there too, like this is not negotiable.

'I don't know how I can make any plans.' I sigh, feeling the dreaminess edge towards harsh reality. 'I need to talk to people, see if I can transfer from coaching in Adelaide to coaching in Melbourne, or maybe there's something else I can do there. I don't know.'

When I first spoke his hands tightened, then loosened before stopping completely. Now they only touch the rounded muscles of my calves.

'Is that not what you want to hear?' I ask with a soft but defensive tone.

He squeezes my calves before his hands leave me. Then they're on my shoulders, rolling me over, lifting me against him, holding me.

'It's something I dreamed of hearing but not what I expected.' He brushes his lips across the top of my head, over my temple and down my cheek. 'You'd move?' His tongue flicks against the corner of my mouth and mine brushes against it.

Lifting my hand until it curls over his jaw and cheek, I stroke softly. Our lips meet in a single chaste kiss.

Gentle fingers stroke me. A brush across my cheekbone. One finger glides over the swell of my breast and across my ever-tightening nipple. A hand closes over my hipbone before easing down my thigh. Lips graze my neck, collarbone, cleavage.

I'm rendered immobile. Unable to lift a hand to touch him. Not through anything he's done to restrain me but through the lassitude brought about by his touch, our talk today, and everything that's happened since I met him.

I'm doing a jigsaw in my head, working through my churning thoughts and feelings, trying to work out logistics. And while my brain is busy, he worships me.

There's no other way to describe the reverence of his touch, the sensitivity of his tasting, the sanctuary of his body. I soak up his devotion, allowing it to soothe my fractured mind. Goosebumps follow his mouth. Prickling heralds his hand. My body comes alive, even as my brain fumbles and flusters.

His hands slide down to my knees, calves, feet, and his mouth follows the downward movement, trailing the slope of breast to ribs and stomach. Kisses press to my left hip bone as his fingers stroke the top of my feet and massage each toe.

His mouth moves from left hip bone to right, nose brushing the sensitive skin below my navel. A moan pushes upwards and expels through my parted lips.

He kisses my right hip bone, licking delicately across the point.

His hands slide up my legs, thumbs stroking the backs of my knees until bubbles fill my bloodstream and I feel like I've drunk too much champagne. Then he pushes my thighs apart as he strokes the flesh up and down, up and down, mesmerising me with the rhythm, the tune, the touch.

His mouth finds my slick folds. Tongue probes and parts. My legs slightly buckle, dipping, spreading wider. I arch my back and my hips push into his face. The rhythm of his lapping never wavers. His lips flutter across my clit, opening me wider with their pressure.

Hard fingers curl into my upper thighs, holding me with their strength and giving me a focus aside from the pleasure from his mouth.

I concentrate on the sting of my flesh beneath his gripping fingers and there's a glimpse of sanity, a break from the sex-spell. I can lift my hands, run my fingers across the top of his head with the short hair tickling the pads of my fingertips and the sides of my fingers. My fingers tingle, the sensation racing up my arms and through my chest. My cunt quivers with longing, sending shards of need through my stomach and higher. The waves of need meet in my chest, producing waves twice the size of the original. Waves of pleasure thrum me.

When his tongue probes my core and thrusts into me, I grab the sides of his head, his ears hot against my palms.

'God, Coop. Yes.' I've found my voice in time for an orgasm to scream from my body. His mouth flutters against my clit while he tongue-fucks me, and it brings me undone. Breaks me, cell by cell.

As I'm pulsing and throbbing, gasping for breath, he picks me up and lifts me onto the edge of the bed. Striding between my thighs, he elevates my legs and spears me with his cock. A deep growl rumbles through his body before being emitted into the electrified air around us.

His cock surges inside and pulsing waves of orgasm continue to pound me. Each thrust sends me higher, riding waves of euphoria. Each withdrawal is a moment where my body stiffens in fear or anticipation, which only makes the following thrust more intense, more euphoric, more ... more ... Just more.

I'm screaming inside, gasping for air, as orgasm after orgasm cascades through me. A few quick hard thrusts and Cooper floods me, his body arching as his groan drowns my noise.

He holds my hips tightly, holds me to him, holds me as if he's never going to let me go. His body shakes and trembles but that may only be me wobbling.

When the world stills and my lungs have sufficient oxygen, our gazes meet and lock. A sheen covers his eyes and I imagine mine must look the same. It's a different feeling to today's orgasm on the beach where tears fell. This one's a less open, but somehow deeper emotion altogether. Something raw and rich. Both gut-churning and elating. Something that floods my soul and thrills my heart. Something that makes me lean close and smile before I whisper against his lips, 'I love you, Coop.' No fear comes with the words. My chest swells with happiness.

He captures my mouth, lifts me and holds me against him. His cock slips from inside me and I feel bereft, but the way he holds me tight overrides the sense of loss. He folds us both onto the cushioning softness. All the while he kisses me with such tenderness and passion.

When the kiss breaks, he strokes my cheek. 'Thank you, Sam.' He holds me against him, aligned to him perfectly. My feet against his feet. My knees opposite his knees, my hips at his hips, his cock nestled against my pubic bone and abdomen, my breasts against his chest. His arms are wrapped around me, holding me close. I know my eyelids are drooping, as if today's emotion has taken everything out of me. I'm struggling to stay awake.

My eyelids open and I catch his gaze, holding it tightly with mine. 'I promise I'll get things sorted and move to Melbourne. I won't let you down.'

He kisses both my eyelids. 'I know you won't. I promise to fit you into my life. Other guys do, so can I. We'll make this work.'

And we will.

***

At the airport the next morning, the real world wallops me hard. I'm leaving. I've made promises, as has he, but we'll be apart and it's easier to let things slide when you aren't with someone physically. I need to give him an out.

But there's goddamn people everywhere. I don't want this conversation overheard.

'Want to get some fresh air while we wait?'

When Cooper nods, I lead him outside away from the crowd. Folding my arms across my chest, I stand and face him. 'I haven't really won anything. You've beaten me each time. So I'm not holding you to anything—'

'You won three photos and the swim.'

I look at him sceptically. 'How convenient to grant them to me now.' I grin to soften the chastisement.

He looks at me seriously, with concern. 'I thought the competition between us was different to us being together?'

I bite my lips together and will myself to say what I must. 'Yes, but if you change your mind about us, I won't hold you to it.'

'I won't be changing my mind. Are you?' His stare is so intense. I can't break it as I shake my head.

He leans close and whispers right into my ear so no one can possibly overhear. 'You won the most important thing, Sam.'

I pull away slightly, enough to breathe and think. What did I win? Does he mean the overall photo? My face scrunches as I try to work it out. Cooper smiles. This smile's a cross between the Madonna's and the Cheshire Cat's. I give up trying to work it out. 'What?'

He presses fingers over my lips, then leans close. His tongue flicks against my ear lobe before his lips brush my ear. His breath is warm and moist, sending shudders through me. One hand slides along my folded forearms, stroking and kneading. His other arm curls around my shoulders. I'm surrounded, held. I close my eyes to savour the moment.

'You won me, Sam. I love you.' His words are softly whispered against my ear. So soft they take an age to penetrate into the processing unit in my brain. When they're deciphered, my body melts. My lips pull into the largest grin, so large my cheeks hurt, in the best way possible. I lean against him, soaking into him. He could not have said anything more perfect.

From the corner of my eye, my worst fear materialises. The news man. His camera. Snapping photos. Of us.

Cooper moves. He must feel the tension in me. The news man comes bounding to us and I feel Cooper's groan in a gust of air against my cheek.

'Cooper, I thought you two were competitors. This looks like something so much more.' He's grimacing as if he's been cheated. As if Cooper lied. As if our business is his. It grates on my nerves.

I swing from Cooper's arms and stare at the reporter. 'Mate, have you never heard of a goodbye kiss and a holiday fling? Piss off and leave us alone.'

His face goes from shock, to horror, to amazement, to dismay in the space of seconds. He glances at Cooper who says nothing, his face a stony mask.

'Sorry. I thought maybe there was a story here. I'll leave you then.' He makes his way back to the terminal while I mutter every swear word I know under my breath.

I swing back to Cooper, my hand flat against his chest.

'We back to the holiday fling, Sam?' A coldness clings to the question, making me frown.

'What?' I look into Cooper's tense face. I grab his jaw between my hands and plant a big kiss on the thin straight line of his lips. 'No way.' I nuzzle his mouth with little kisses. 'You see, this sexy hot guy taught me to only give 'em a little part of myself. So that's all I gave him.' My kiss deepens, my tongue brushes across his lips, touching between them briefly before I pull away. 'The rest of me is yours, Coop.'

After a short burst of noise, which could be laughter or a groan, he hugs me close. 'Jesus, Sam. Don't scare me like that. I thought you were serious.'

'I used my most serious voice.'

He shakes his head while grinning. 'First you accost me with a wolf-whistle. Then you knock my rule book out of play. Now you're accosting journos. You're going to take some getting used to, Samantha Caine.'

'I love to keep a man on his toes.'

The kiss we share is filled with love, hope, joy and promise. Walking onto the aircraft, I turn and wave, catching the kisses he blows for the world to see. Luckily the news man is paying no attention.

I'm walking towards the future. It will be a challenge. But there's nothing I love more than a challenge. Except Cooper.

BESTSELLING TITLES BY ESCAPE PUBLISHING...

The Virginity Mission
Cate Ellink

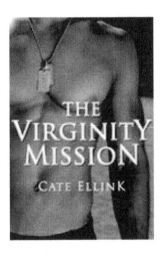

An erotic new adult romance about old insecurities, new beginnings, and the things you can get up to in a tent...

It's lust at first sight when Mac sees Jason shirtless and sweating on the back of a truck. Jason is the army sergeant assigned to support the six week scientific expedition that Mac is participating in, and might just be the perfect candidate for another journey of discovery that Mac is desperate to undertake—sex.

Fraternisation between students and staff might be strictly prohibited, but everybody knows fruit always tastes better when it's forbidden.

Sky High, Bone Deep
N.M. Harris

Traditionally, leather is an anniversary gift. One couple is about to take that in a very non-traditional way...

Rory and Lily have been married for five years, and they have special plans to celebrate their anniversary: a little game involving a collar and a leash and some silky underwear ... for Rory. A little light bondage can be just for fun—but beyond the play, there is love, bone deep and bright as the stars.

Release
Elizabeth Dunk

Four stories of eroticism, strength, experimentation, and ultimate salvation.

Cursed after death to live in grey nothingness until they atone for their sins, four spirits have spent centuries doing good for others. Finally they stumble upon the true key to their salvation—because they hurt women in their lives, they'll only find release by now helping women to become all they should be.

One by one, the spirits meet a woman and as each sexual delight unfurls, the grey nothingness disappears a little more. As the women find their happily ever after, they grant the spirits a chance at peace for eternity.

Follow the journey of four remarkable women—Luisa, Anna, Cara, and Jan—and the four spirits that set them on a new path to sexual freedom and boundless pleasure.

Connect with us for info on our new releases, access to exclusive offers, free online reads and much more!

Sign up to our newsletter

Share your reading experience on:

The Escapades Blog

Facebook

Twitter

Watch our reviews, author interviews and more on *Escape Publishing TV*